THE CWTCH INN CHRISTMAS

by

Peter Lawson
with
contributions from
Andrew P.Lawson

Email : petelookout@hotmail.com

CONTENTS

CHAPTER ONE
CHRISTMAS PREPARATIONS ARE IN HAND

There were six days to go before Christmas, and the owners of the Cwtch Inn, Henry and Myfannwy Griffiths, were continuing with their arrangements to receive their guests for Christmas. Their daughter Claire, the Inn's resident chef, and their staff of five, were also busily gearing up for the days ahead. The Cwtch Inn, popularly known just as the 'Cwtch', was nestled in a small valley to the North of Cardiff and situated on the outskirts of the small village of Pontynant.

Henry, Myfannwy and Claire had decided to restrict the number of guests this Christmas in order that refurbishment work could be carried out on the various chalets dotted around the forty-acre site. The inn was expecting its first guests that very day from the United States and Norway. Their American guests, comprising of a family of three from Pennsylvania, and their Norwegian guests, a family of three from Oslo, were to be the only scheduled guests being catered for. However, what they did not know was there were unexpected guests heading their way!

Their plans and those of the local vicar, Patsy, involved holding various events over the course of the upcoming days, but little could anyone predict the unexpected and magical events that were about to weave their way into the fabric of their intentions.

CHAPTER TWO
THE AMERICANS ARE COMING

With an ultimate destination of Milford Haven in West Wales, the Intercity 125 had left London Paddington on time, and was now a mere half an hour from Cardiff. It was early afternoon and aboard the train, sitting in the first-class compartment, was the Bidder family from the United States of America.

They had flown over from the States that very morning and all were showing signs of being tired. They were to be met at Cardiff railway station by Henry and his general handyman Bob and, once on board the minibus, they were to be transported the short distance to the Cwtch.

John Bidder, a fifty-year old restaurateur, and his wife Cynthia were travelling with their twenty four-year old son Joseph to Wales for the first time. Their restaurant back in Pennsylvania was being looked after by Luigi, John's elder brother and head chef. Joseph would be the first to admit that his own success as a chef in the restaurant was down to the talent and mentoring of his uncle Luigi.

John was gazing through the compartment window and contemplating the hoped-for relaxation that the stay at the inn would bring. It had been a long but prosperous year for the Bidder restaurant and John had concluded that the three of them deserved this break. Cynthia had concurred with her husband on the merits of the trip, but Joseph had been rather reluctant to pack his cases. Cynthia who had been digesting the contents of the inn's brochure and an accompanying letter from Henry Griffiths placed these down on the table in front of her when John turned towards them to talk.

'Have you both recovered from the flight?' he asked, yawning slightly himself.

Cynthia was the first to respond by saying that she had almost, but she was looking forward to getting a good night's sleep. John turned to Joe for his response. Joe folded the newspaper he had been reading and put it on the seat next to him.

'You know my feelings Dad. I really wanted to stay home and spend Christmas with the family and all my friends.'

'I know' his father replied, 'but this was the only opportunity we had to take this vacation and your mother and I really wanted you to have a rest from work and unwind with us.'

Cynthia added. 'You've been working your socks off for the last six months in the kitchen with your Uncle Luigi. You deserve this vacation.'

'I know, and look guys, I have no intention of spoiling this holiday. Once I get into the rhythm of things, I'll be okay.' His father looking more reassured by his son's words, smiled, and responded by saying. 'It might end up with you being glad you came and who knows what, we might have a lot of fun.'

Cynthia pointed to the brochure and letter in front of her and commented, 'Judging by what I have read in the brochure and Mr. Griffiths' letter there's going to be a lot going on, but if Joseph, you want to just laze around you can, and don't forget, we can always do some on site family research.' Cynthia paused for a moment and then continued.

'What did Henry Griffiths sound like when you spoke to him on the phone last week, John?'

'Cynthia. He was one of the friendliest sounding people I have encountered for a while. I think we are going to get on with him and his family. Bye the way Joe, his daughter Claire is your age and apparently unattached.'

Joe quickly replied that it was probably because she was not the best catch in the world. Regardless, he was not prepared to think about romantic entanglements at this time. His mother pointed out that they had their love of cooking in common, to which Joe said in reply. 'I would like to spend some time in her kitchen to see what a Welsh kitchen is all about and how it compares to our kitchen, but that's as far as it goes.'

His father interjected by suggesting that Joe needed therefore to get on her good side. Joe looked at his father and smiled. 'I'm going to be friendly to everyone equally.' he proclaimed.

Meanwhile, Henry and Bob had left the Cwtch in the minibus and were heading towards Cardiff to pick up their American guests. Henry, now in his mid-fifties, had inherited the one-time country manor from his father and had, with the support of his family and workforce, developed the business to encompass not just the main inn building, but the several chalets in the grounds. He was being accompanied on this trip by his main handyman Bob. Bob had worked for the Cwtch for ten years since the age of twenty-five.

He had jumped at the chance of being a passenger in the minibus with Henry on this trip to Cardiff as he was eager to meet Americans in the flesh. He had, after all, watched many hundreds of them in the American television shows that he spent hours watching. It was this eagerness that prompted Bob's first question. 'Do you think the Americans will wear those funny hats, Henry?' he asked.

Henry was about to reply but was interrupted by his mobile

phone ringing. As Henry was driving, he instructed Bob to pick the phone up and answer it. Bob did so with the words,

'This is the Cwtch Inn minibus here. Henry Griffiths is driving now, so this is his assistant Robert Evans esquire speaking.' Henry stopped him and told him just to say hello. Bob did as he was instructed.

'It's Myfannwy, Henry.'

'Put it on speaker, Bob.'

'Hello Myfannwy. Yes. We are well on our way. Is everything okay back there?'

Myfannwy replied by saying that it was and then asked Henry to confirm that he had spoken to Sammy the Skip. She wanted to ensure that the rubbish filled skip sitting in the inn's yard would be collected without fail before Christmas. Henry confirmed that he had spoken to Sammy and he had received Sammy's promise that it would be. Henry went on to say that he had been listening to the weather forecast and there seemed to be no likelihood of snow for the Christmas.

Myfannwy confirmed that the Christmas tree for the reception had finally been delivered and Kenneth, aided by Gregor, would be erecting it shortly. Kenneth was the bartender and waiter at the inn and Gregor, GG to his friends, was the second handyman and electrician. Henry expressed his relief at the tree being on site and imparted to Myfannwy the necessity for it to be in place and decorated by the time they returned to the Cwtch with their guests.

Having given these snippets of information to Myfannwy, Henry said goodbye and Bob ended the call. Henry turned his head towards Bob and said, 'You were saying about their hats,

Bob.'

'Well on the television I've seen them wearing all sorts of funny hats. Some wear big cowboy hats and some of their hats are made from skunk.'

'I wouldn't worry about their hats. By the way, when we meet our American friends just be your natural self, okay? Let them adjust to you and no American expressions when you meet them. Understand?' Bob nodded.

Back on the train the Bidders had been discussing how they were going to undertake further family research whilst in Wales when the rattle of the refreshment trolley sounded a little way down the corridor. In an instant the trolley, being pushed by its attendant, appeared next to them.

'Hello and good afternoon to you. My name is Sue. Would you like anything off the trolley, today?' Cynthia asked for three coffees, two with cream, one straight black and as she was doing this Sue was listening closely to her accent.

'I'm Cynthia by the way, this is my husband John and my son, Joseph.'

'Now, I'm guessing you are from the U.S.A. by that accent. Am I right?" she asked this as she started to pour the drinks. Cynthia confirmed that they were indeed from the States but added that there were a great many people that could not tell the difference between the American and Canadian accents. Sue pointed out that her many years on the trains had given her the edge but placing the accent to a particular part of a country was still a challenge.

Joe joined the conversation by saying that they hailed from Snow Valley in Pennsylvania. John added that they were over here for the holidays, to relax and take it easy, but also to undertake some family research as his great grandfather had been a Welsh miner who had emigrated to the States way back when. 'We are looking forward to the legendary Welsh hospitality that we've heard so much about.'

Sue answered by saying that was a certainty. She and her husband were from Yorkshire but had spent several holidays in both North and South Wales. Referring to John's comment on his great grandfather she pointed out that most mines had now shut down and Wales was now even greener as a result. 'The Welsh have a saying' she said, 'that there would be a welcome in the hillsides and an even bigger one awaited them because of their Welsh connection.'

'They have their own language don't they?' asked Joe.

'They do, but a large majority speak English, so you have nothing to be concerned about there.'

Joe then changed the subject completely by asking if Sue had any pistachio nuts on her trolley, but she had not.

She did suggest that there may be some in the buffet bar in the next carriage. Joe thanked her and headed off in that direction. Sue finished pouring the drinks, wished the Bidders a merry Christmas, and pushed her trolley further down the compartment.

CHAPTER THREE
THE WELSH PISTACHIO LADY

Joe entered the buffet bar area with an eagerness to obtain his favourite snack, the humble pistachio nut. He arrived at the counter as the attendant was finishing serving another passenger and just a second or two before a young lady, who had come from the compartment further down the train. Unbeknown to Joe she was in fact Elizabeth, Henry Griffiths' second daughter. Moreover, as Joe would eventually discover, she was Claire's identical twin.

Elizabeth was travelling to initially meet friends in Swansea and subsequently go home to the Cwtch for an unannounced Christmas visit. She was accompanied on the journey by her fiancé Gerald. Joe, although before Elizabeth in the queue, took a step backwards to allow her to go first. With the proper gesture of his hand to beckon her forward he said 'Please, you go ahead.'

'Thank you.' replied Elizabeth who then faced the attendant and asked if he had a packet of salted peanuts. He replied that he did not have any salted peanuts left, but he did have one last packet of pistachio nuts under the counter. At this Joe exclaimed 'Oh!'. Elizabeth turned to face him to see why he had uttered these words. She enquired as to what the problem was.

'You say you only have the one packet? Joe asked the attendant.

'Yes sir. Only the one.'

Then looking at Elizabeth, Joe informed her that pistachios

were his favourite snack. He said this just as the attendant passed the packet to Elizabeth.

'You did say I could go first!' Elizabeth pointed out.

'Sure did, but say, could we not share the packet?'

The attendant interjected and suggested that sharing the packet would resolve the issue. He offered up two plastic cups for the division. Elizabeth politely thanked him for his suggestion but, on this occasion, she was not prepared to relinquish possession of them.

'I thought you English liked us Americans,' said Joe, 'and I am after all I am a visitor to your country.'

Elizabeth looked at him with a somewhat icy stare. 'I will respond to that with two comments. One, I am not English. I am Welsh. Second, I do like most Americans but clearly there is at least one that I am taking a disliking to.' Joe replied to this by asking whether the twang in her voice was a Welsh one.

'A Twang? You can talk with that American accent!' she retorted. 'Anyway, I need to go back to my companions and share these pistachios with them.' As she turned away Joe commented that regardless of anything, her Christmas hat was cute, too big for her, but cute.

She replied 'waeth beth fo' which Joe took to be an insult. He did not know that it just simply meant whatever. As she walked away, but with her still being in earshot, Joe said he was going to call her the Welsh Pistachio Lady as he had not found out what her real name was. Elizabeth called back, 'and you will not hear that from me, that's for sure! Goodbye American.'

Joe was intrigued as to what waeth beth fo meant and posed

the question to the attendant. 'Do you know what waeth beth fo means?' The attendant replied that he had not got a clue. He was from Barnsley. Joe settled on having a bag of crisps and returned to his compartment.

When he arrived back in his seat his mother questioned why he had changed his mind over the pistachios. Joe explained that the Welsh pistachio lady had secured the last packet. Having said that he was committed to telling them that he had apparently upset the first Welsh person he had met.

Cynthia was disappointed at hearing this, but John asked whether she was pretty. Joe, who had found the young lady attractive, commented that he had not really noticed. His father smiled, Joe smiled, and his mother suggested that he not upset any more individuals.

A short while later the train pulled into Cardiff railway station on time and the Bidders alighted the train complete with luggage. They stood for a while on the platform, waited for the other passengers to leave, and watched the train gently pull away on its onward journey westward.

As the last compartment was passing them Joe spotted his Welsh pistachio lady still wearing her Christmas hat, and with the pistachio packet in hand, looking out of the window.

Joe caught her attention, waved and gave her a smile. Elizabeth did not respond other than to place another pistachio in her mouth and show that she was really enjoying it. Joe did not have any further chance to respond to this as the train had pulled away.

CHAPTER FOUR
THE FIRST STAGE OUT OF TOWN

The Cwtch minibus arrived at the station carpark with minutes to spare, and after several attempts to find a parking bay, Henry finally managed to secure a spot close to the main station exit to the annoyance of the taxi drivers. Henry and Bob decided to stand by the side of the minibus to get a better view. It was probably the stature of Bob that persuaded the taxi drivers to keep their distance. It was however only a matter of moments after parking up that the Bidders approached.

John was the first to speak. 'Hi there! I guess you are here to pick us up. We are the Bidders.'

Henry responded with a broad smile, the Welsh welcome of croeso, and 'We certainly are. I am Henry Griffiths, and this is Bob. I am assuming you are John, this is your wife Cynthia, and this is your son Joseph.' Joe said he preferred to be called Joe.

After the formalities of shaking hands and introductions Henry invited the Bidders to hop on board the minibus whilst he and Bob loaded the luggage. Bob had forgotten what Henry had said about expressions by welcoming the Bidders with a big 'Howdy pardners.'

Cynthia was about to climb into the minibus when Bob, putting three cases back on the floor, took her arm and said, 'Let me help you get safely on the stage, Mrs. Bidder.' He emphasised the word stage and Henry shook his head in disbelief. With everyone onboard Henry weaved the minibus out through the taxi drivers in the rank and negotiated his way out of the carpark. The journey to the Cwtch had begun.

With his passengers safely onboard and settled, Henry asked if they had recovered from their journey thus far, to which Joe replied that they seemed to be fine, but they had all agreed a good night's sleep was the order of the day later. Cynthia expressed her excitement at the prospect of staying at the inn and this prompted John to ask what the word cwtch meant.

Henry replied that it meant to cuddle. Henry explained that when his father developed the inn, he wanted it to be a place that offered up a warm welcome to all its guests to which Cynthia commented that it was to be a place that 'liked to cuddle its guests'. Henry wholeheartedly agreed with that sentiment.

'How long have you been at the Cwtch, Henry?' asked John.

'All my life, John. When my father passed away Myfannwy and I inherited the Cwtch. We have been running it ever since.'

'Myfannwy sounds like a Welsh name, am I right?' asked Cynthia, 'It's certainly a beautiful name.'

'It is, isn't it?' answered Henry, 'Translated, it means my little one.'

'Do you have any children, Henry?' asked John.

'Myfannwy and I have two daughters. Claire and Elizabeth. Claire is the chef at the Cwtch. My other daughter, Elizabeth, decided that working at the Cwtch was not for her but acting was. She is on the London stage at present, would you believe! She can act, sing and dance. In fact, she is as talented when it comes to that as Claire is at cooking. What about you? Any other offspring?'

Joe replied by saying that he had one sister. She lived on

the west coast of the States. He went onto say that every other Christmas she visited them in Snow Valley. Cynthia asked if Elizabeth would be home for Christmas.

'She comes home for the occasional Christmas.' Henry replied. 'Her career has prevented it being an annual occurrence and, judging by what she was saying on the phone the other day, it seemed unlikely that they would be seeing her this year.'

Little did he know that this was not going to be the case. Cynthia commented that this was a shame. She went on to divulge that Claire was indeed her own middle name and that it meant God's grace. Cynthia had been given that middle name after John's great grandmother.

'I don't know whether Dad has told you, Henry,' Joe said, 'but Dad has Welsh ancestors. Dad's great grandfather and great grandmother were born in Wales.'

'Were they indeed?' Henry's eyes lit up at hearing this. 'In that case then we have an extra special welcome in the hillside for you.'

'But what about me, Henry?' asked Cynthia. 'I do not have Welsh blood coursing through my veins.'

'Cynthia, there is an equally warm welcome for you. You had the sense to marry a man who has Welsh blood in his veins.' Cynthia thanked him for this.

Bob then asked John where his ancestors had lived. John explained that they had discovered that Bidders had been, and were still, in all parts of South Wales, particularly Swansea and West Wales but his own great grandfather, Cledwyn and his great grandmother Claire, hailed from a place called Tongwynlais. John's attempt at pronouncing this word was remarkably good. Henry pointed out that Tongwynlais was just a matter of miles from the Cwtch.

'That's partially why we chose your inn.' commented John 'We are doing some family research and hope to pay a visit there, time permitting.' John went on to say that Cledwyn and Claire had been childhood sweethearts and married in Wales back in the day. Cledwyn was a miner and he and Claire emigrated to Pennsylvania when they were both in their twenties. He was well known in his village and indeed he, and one of his four brothers, had fierce-some reputations for fighting in the illegal boxing booths of the time. His nickname was Cledwyn the Clout, and his brother was known as Billy the Bash.'

Bob added that they were hard men in those days, particularly the ones that fought bare fisted and worked in the mines. He himself, even though he was well over 6 feet in height and seventeen stone in weight, thought a gentler life was for him. John asked him whether he liked working at the Cwtch. Bob replied that it was the best job he had ever had even though he originally wanted to follow in his father's footsteps.

Joe asked him what his father did, to which Bob replied that he trained whales. John asked him which national team he coached. Bob clarified his answer by saying that he worked at Sea Escape in Florida, training whales. Bob went on to say that his father had been given the honour of naming two of the whales.

'The park authorities wanted to call them Shampoo or something like that.' he said. Cynthia, somewhat hesitantly, asked Bob what were the names that his father chose. Bob replied that his father had named them Buttercup and Jemima.

Joe, trying hard to hide his amusement, commented that they were certainly names that suited two killer whales. He commented that it must have been a difficult and dangerous job. Bob replied that it must have been given that his father could not swim and that he was allergic to anything from the ocean that was bigger than a sardine. John, Joe and Sylvia smiled and Henry shook his head.

'Bob is a character, isn't he?' said Henry. 'Talking about characters I have to say that we have several characters in the village.'

CHAPTER FIVE
AGGIE MEETS MAGGIE

At the very time that Henry was mentioning the characters that lived in the village, two of those very individuals were meeting in the main street of Pontynant. Aggie and Maggie were both in their early sixties and both were regarded as being somewhat eccentric, eccentric but harmless. Aggie greeted Maggie first.

'Hello Maggie.'

'Hello Aggie. How's Dougie, Aggie?'

'He's his normal self, Maggie.'

'That's a shame Aggie.'

'I haven't seen Margie lately, Maggie.'

'Mum hasn't been too well lately, Aggie. She is in her nineties now remember. Poor old plum pudding, isn't it?'

'Is she still frightening the cats?'

'She's never stopped. With a face like hers, what else? Cats won't go near the nursing home now!'

'Hereditary, I guess. Still, I half expect her to fly in on her broomstick any moment.'

'Perhaps she will! Then again, the problem is that I do not think she has any broomsticks. I think they were all confiscated, isn't it?'

Their conversation was interrupted by the arrival of one of the local club's rugby players out on a training run. Steve ran towards them in his rugby kit and, as he passed, Maggie shouted, 'Hey Steve. I've seen better looking legs on my deckchair, if I had a deckchair that is.'

Steve was quick to reply with, 'And I have seen a better-looking face on a turnip. See you Maggie.' Maggie replied, 'See you Steve', and turning to Aggie said, 'Well I must be off. See you Aggie.' Aggie replied with 'See you Maggie.'

Meanwhile back in the minibus Henry was explaining further that there were certainly quite a few characters in the village but regardless, it was a very pleasant village to be part of. John asked how many people lived in the village. Henry had to think for a moment but answered that there was about one hundred. This prompted Cynthia to ask how many guests would be in the Cwtch for the Christmas.

Henry replied that in addition to Cynthia and her family there was another family of three coming over from Norway. Henry explained to them about the refurbishment programme that was taking place. Henry looked at the clock on the dashboard and said that in fact the Norwegians should have left the ferry terminal and be on their way by road to South Wales.

This was indeed the case. Asgard Larsen, a schoolteacher and cabbage grower, with his wife Sofie and their ten-year old daughter Ingrid, had cleared customs and were on route in their Volvo. The Larsens were determined that to improve their English they would speak it during their entire stay in the U.K. Asgard said that he was really looking forward to this Christmas vacation to which both Sofie and Ingrid wholeheartedly agreed.

Ingrid, an extremely keen photographer, held up her camera and said that it was her intention to take many photographs during her time in Wales. Sofie turned to her husband and asked,

'Do you think Mr. Griffiths will have ordered sufficient cabbage, Asgard?'

'I hope so, but just in case I have brought thirty of my best Norwegian King cabbages with us.' This was indeed the case as these cabbages were now in a large net secured to the roof of the Volvo.

'Yes indeed', said Henry back in the minibus, 'the Norwegian family will complete our international family at the Cwtch, and as we are all going to be within the main building it should be very cosy.' Henry paused for a moment and then continued, 'and I think you will love Claire's cooking. She is an excellent chef.'

'It sounds like', Cynthia began, 'that we did make the right decision to come here for our vacation, John.' She paused momentarily.' I understand that Claire is single, Henry.' Joe looked at his mother hoping she would not go further but she did. 'Of course, Joseph is single also.'

'And they would be about the same age, wouldn't they?' Henry asked. 'Claire had a boyfriend up until last year, but he moved to Australia. Perhaps Joe and Claire would be good company for each other over the next week or so.'

Joe put a stop to this conversation. 'Hold your horses, both of you! No match making right?'

Sensing that they had hit a nerve, Henry said 'I'm pleased to hear that you think you have made the right decision to come here, Cynthia. By the way, what do you folks do back in

Pennsylvania?' Joe, eager to steer the conversation in that direction, replied that they owned and ran the family restaurant in a place called Snow Valley. All the family were involved in the business with his Uncle Luigi being the head chef.

Cynthia added more detail by saying that out of Luigi and Joseph, Joseph was the more adventurous of the two in the kitchen, John was the administrator and business brains, but she was the ultimate person in control. Henry sensed that Joe and his father were not going to argue with her last comment.

John turned to Bob and asked whether he was a married man. Bob replied that he was not, that the right girl had not yet found him. He went on to say. 'I came close though. My first girlfriend Wendy and I were about to become engaged, but she wanted to pursue her dream of tracking down the Yeti.' The mention of the Yeti really caught the attention of the Bidders. 'One day she packed her bags and just left. The intention was for me to follow her out there, but I didn't.'

'Why ever not?' asked Cynthia.

'I concluded that pursuing a strange and smelly creature out there was just not for me.'

'But how did you know the Yeti was strange and smelly?' asked Joe.

'I was talking about Wendy!' Bob replied.

John said 'That's a great joke, Bob. You had us going there.'

Henry interjected. 'Trouble is John, he was serious.'

Cynthia, trying to change the subject as quickly as possible, asked Henry if there was any likelihood of there being snow in the forthcoming days. Henry updated her on this by saying that it was highly unlikely. Cynthia expressed some disappointment as she would have loved some. Bob asked if Snow Valley got any snow.

Joe, still trying to recover from the Wendy story, said that 'back home' was in the middle of a blizzard. Bob asked how they coped, and Joe pointed out that the local authorities had some really, big, mean snow ploughs and blowers. Joe asked how they managed at the inn when it snowed.

Henry answered this proudly. 'We have Bob!' The Bidders looked collectively surprised at this. 'Oh yes! Big Bob here, with his bucket and spade, is the man for the job.' Cynthia queried this but Bob replied that it was correct. After all it was a big spade.

CHAPTER SIX
THIS YEAR'S CHRISTMAS TREE

Back at the Cwtch, James, the local Christmas tree grower, had indeed delivered the tree that was to take pride of place in the reception area of the inn. Such was the demand for trees this year that James was a good two days behind with his deliveries. Myfannwy had supervised the delivery and inspected the tree to ensure that it was right in all aspects. Fortunately for James it was.

Myfannwy had immediately called Gregor, the inn's Polish handyman and electricia, from the workshop and, with Kenneth also enlisted, she charged them with their task and gave them the deadline for completion. She also reminded them that within that deadline the Father Christmas, polar bear and snowman were also to be fully inflated with the helium she had bought for them, and they too had to be placed in the reception hall.

Having given them their orders, Myfannwy, accompanied by Claire, left the inn to visit Patsy the local vicar and to do some shopping in the village. As they passed through reception on their way out Myfannwy reassured Sandra on reception that they would return in time to greet their guests.

The tree, which had been resting on its side in the reception hall was soon standing upright in its bespoke metal stand. Sandra had left her desk and approached Kenneth and Gregor. Jokingly she said that at least they had the tree the right way up. Both Kenneth and Gregor knew she was pulling their legs. She told them that their task was only half complete though. The decorations needed to be put on the tree and the mess cleared up.

At the mention of decorations Kenneth looked at Gregor and asked where the decorations were. Gregor did not know, and both immediately developed worried expressions. Sandra found this very amusing and could not resist delaying telling them that she had secreted the decorations under her reception desk. She enjoyed the moment for a while and then let the cat out of the bag. Gregor and Kenneth were more relieved than angry, however. She brought them over to them and said, 'Now be careful with these!'

Kenneth said that she should have more faith in them, and Gregor thought it would be a good idea to turn the tables on Sandra by suggesting that the tree needed to be nailed to the floor. Sandra took the bait and warned hm not to do that. Henry and Myfannwy would kill him. Gregor smiled and Sandra realised that she had been taken in.

'Always the joker!' Sandra walked away shaking her head.

Half an hour later, the tree was fully adorned with decorations and lights. The two stepped backwards to admire their work at the same time as Sandra came over to inspect.

'You've done quite a good job there, boys,' she said, 'but you'd better hurry now and clear up your mess.'

Gregor, in response to this instruction, said to Kenneth in polish, 'She nags like my wife.' Sandra did not understand this but did realise that because he was talking in Polish it had to be derogatory. He went on to fib by saying that it meant 'you light up my day with your presence.'

Sandra looked at him, smiled and in Welsh said, 'you are the proof that evolution can work backwards.' That means Gregor that 'I am all the better for knowing you.' The clear up was completed and they all retired to the kitchen for a quick cup of tea.

Their task was, after all, only half done. The polar bear, Father Christmas and the snowman awaited them. Little could they predict the problems that these inanimate objects would present.

After their short tea break, Sandra, Gregor and Kenneth were back in the reception hall. Gregor had retrieved the three inflatables from their storage place in one of the cupboards and Kenneth had brought in the helium gas cylinder. Sandra remembered that last year they had to secure extra weights to the inflatables because their own internal weights were inadequate, but Gregor had pre-empted this, and proudly presented his weight-lifting weights as the solution.

In addition, Kenneth went to ensure that the front doors were securely shut. He came back and commented how windy it was outside and that they certainly would have to tie the inflatables down securely. Inflating the three models took only a few minutes and positioning the extra weights out of sight did not present any problems.

However, Sandra's observation that the string they were using looked too thin was ruled out by the other two. Gregor, to pacify her, agreed to double up on the lengths of string.

What did cause a delay in the proceedings was the conversation that took place as to the type of knot that was to be used. Kenneth, a keen angler, managed to persuade the others that his ability in this field would give them the perfect knot. Job done, the three admired their handywork and decided to have another tea break.

They proceeded accordingly to the kitchen leaving the

Father Christmas, snowman and polar bear all seemingly happy to be back out of storage. Sandra had commented on how the three inflatables had such happy faces.

Having retired to the kitchen it was only a matter of moments before the wind blew open the front doors and the inflatables began to pull on their restraints. Ignorant of these goings on Sandra instructed Gregor and Kenneth not to tell Maggie, on any account, that each of the inflatables had labels saying that they had been manufactured in Llanelli. Realising the consequences if they did, both swore to keep silent.

Meanwhile, one by one, the inflatables were breaking away from their moorings and, with the wind behind them, were floating up the corridor. Both the doubling up of the strings and the choice of knot had failed and they took on the appearance of hot air balloons straining to get off the ground.

CHAPTER SEVEN
THE ECAPEES

The minibus was now approaching the outskirts of Pontynant and Henry informed his passengers that they had almost reached their destination. Soon they would be introduced to the rest of the team and be enjoying a welcome drink in the lounge. Joe asked if they were as friendly as he and Bob. Henry thanked him for making this observation and informed him that he could not be prouder of his team for their friendliness and hard work.

Henry began to describe his employees to Joe. 'Take Sandra for example. She is hardworking and has a very amicable personality. It is rare for her not to have a smile on her face.' Little did Henry know that at that very instant the snowman had managed to tuck itself in behind the reception desk. With a huge 'Sandra-like' smile on its face it was ready to receive its guests.

Henry went on to describe Kenneth. 'Now, Kenneth is our resident bartender. He is able to mix you any drink you care to ask for.' Back at the inn, the Father Christmas, seemingly more adventurous than the snowman, had meandered further down the corridor and had made its way to behind the bar. It, like the snowman, seemed to want to become an employee of the inn and certainly it was enjoying its new role as temporary bartender if its smiling face was anything to go by.

Henry, although mistaken in his belief, suggested that Myfannwy and Claire would, at this time, be busy in the kitchen and Gregor busy in his workshop. Had Myfannwy and Claire been present at the inn the actual circumstances might have been different. However, they were not, and the extended long tea break that the staff were having, allowed the third escapee to wind its way further down the corridor and into the lounge.

Sitting in front of one of the settees and watching the television was Bonnie, the labrador belonging to Bob. She often sat and watched the television when no one was around, and every time Kenneth spotted her in this position, he would turn the television on for her. On this occasion she was, ironically. watching a programme on wildlife.

At first she was taken back by the appearance of the inflatable polar bear, but she had seen it before, and allowed all six feet of it to settle down by her.

What happened next however, was the appearance on the television screen of a pair of polar bears. The programme had started to feature creatures of the Arctic. It was what the narrator said next that Bonnie really took notice of.

'Cute as they may seem, polar bears are extremely dangerous animals. Some people have described them as the great white sharks of the north.'

It was this that made Bonnie retreat to the back of one of the armchairs still looking at the smile that was spread across the polar bear's face.

The minibus was now at the outskirts of the inn. It was late afternoon and darkness was beginning to descend. At the entrance to the property stood the old gatehouse which originally was the reception house for the old country manor. It was now the residence of Bob. Henry noticed that a large plastic rubbish bag had become lodged on the Cwtch Inn sign, so he stopped the minibus in front of the gatehouse and instructed Bob to rectify the situation.

As Bob did so, John, now looking at Cynthia and Joe, commented to Henry that he thought the inn would be a lot bigger. He was almost at the point of saying that they were all a little disappointed when Henry began to laugh. He asked to be excused for laughing and, just as Bob had returned to the minibus, he informed them that it was just the gatehouse. He drove the minibus fifty yards further around the curving drive and then announced,

'This, my friends, is the Cwtch!'

The Cwtch in all its glory was now revealed and even though it was not yet fully dark the Christmas lights that had been strung on it were shining brightly. Cynthia was the first to comment by saying how pretty it was. John and Joe added how it now met and surpassed their expectations.

As the minibus was drawing up in front of the main entrance, Sandra was in reception with Kenneth and Gregor and, having captured their escapees, were now feverishly securing them back in position with extra strong ties and weights. They were in the hall as Henry led the American guests through the front doors.

Henry complimented them on how good a job they had done with the tree and the inflatables and asked whether they had any problems. Sandra gave a sidewise glance to Kenneth and Gregor and replied that everything had gone smoothly. Henry proceeded to introduce his staff to the Bidders and as he was doing so Myfannwy returned to the inn. , who had been unloading the minibus, was now laden down with the shopping that Myfannwy had bought.

Myfannwy welcomed the Bidders to the Cwtch after Henry had introduced her as his lovely wife. She then explained that Claire had stopped off to chat to Patsy, the vicar, and they would meet up with her later. Henry suggested that they could all catch up later in the lounge for a welcome drink but, in the meantime, Sandra would book them in, and Bob and Gregor would take them and their luggage to their rooms.

Bonnie, who had recovered from her encounter with the great white shark, came into the hall, glanced at the polar bear, and introduced herself to the Bidders.

CHAPTER EIGHT
HENRY'S TALE OF MAGICAL VISITORS

That evening, John and Cynthia were introduced to both Claire and the wonderful food she had prepared for them, and having enjoyed their meal in the dining room, they made their way, with Henry and Cynthia, to the lounge to relax. They had been chatting for about ten minutes when Claire came into the lounge with Kenneth.

Between them they were carrying the drinks that had previously been ordered. Kenneth, who had met the Bidders whilst serving wine at dinner, distributed the drinks and then returned to his bar.

John was the first to compliment Claire again on the food they had just consumed. 'I did not realise Claire how hungry I was until I saw and smelt the food you prepared for us. It was delicious. I only wish Joe had made it down. I know he was going to ring his uncle back in Snow Falls to see how things were going there and he did say that if he got the chance, he would do some family research on his computer.'

Cynthia suggested that he may have crashed out as he did look tired after the journey but that he should make it down later. Cynthia added that Claire had served them up a treat of a meal and that she was looking forward to more culinary delights during their stay. Claire replied by saying that there was plenty more to come and that there was plenty left for Joseph when he did make an appearance. She was about to turn and head back to the kitchen when Cynthia asked.

'Are you nearly finished in the kitchen for the night, Claire? I was wondering whether you could join us for a drink.'

'I would love to Cynthia, but I think Molly and I will be clearing up and prepping for tomorrow. It is going to be a late one, but if you are still around when I do finish, I will join you. If I do not, I will see you all in the morning for breakfast.' Claire hastened back to the kitchen leaving her parents to continue chatting with the Bidders.

'When are you expecting your Norwegian guests, Henry?' asked John.

'Actually, they should have been here by now.' was the reply.

'I must say Henry you have a lovely daughter in Claire.' The compliment came from Cynthia.

'Yes, she is a treasure, and she works so hard.' Henry replied.

At this point Joe, accompanied by Bonnie, entered the room.

'Ah, Joseph. You look refreshed.' His mother commented.

'I'm feeling much better after a shower. I am so sorry I missed dinner. Uncle Luigi wouldn't stop asking me questions.'

'How are things back home?' his father enquired.

'They seem to be coping well even though there's still a raging blizzard. Have I completely missed dinner? I can certainly detect some lovely smells coming from somewhere.'

'Claire has left you some dinner in the dining room.' His mother pointed out, 'By the way you have only just missed Claire. She had to go back to the kitchen.'

'Can I get you something from the dining room, Joe? Myfannwy asked.

'No that's okay. I'll go and grab something now.'

Henry caught him before he disappeared. 'And when you come back, I'll fill you and your parents in on a few things.' Joe headed off in the direction of the dining room.

Cynthia looked around the lounge and commented that the Cwtch, despite her having been there a short while, seemed like it had a magical atmosphere. Myfannwy agreed with her and said that the atmosphere was always very pleasant but sometimes it became elevated to another level.

'How so, Myfannwy?' asked John.

'Well, when we have weddings and parties here, the work is demanding, but we have enjoyed it all. Christmas is when feel that the magic really happens, isn't that so, Henry?'

Henry replied that he could not disagree with that and when Joe rejoined them, he would highlight what had been planned for the week. A few minutes later, Joe, carrying a plate of food in one hand and a cup of coffee in the other, rejoined them. Henry told him that they had just been talking about the special atmosphere that pervaded the inn at Christmas and it was no different this year. Joe nodded and dived further into his food.

'Wow!' he exclaimed, 'this sure is excellent food. I hope your daughter will share her recipes with me, Myfannwy. This food is certainly wonderful.'

Myfannwy then said that she had the feeling that something extra special and magical would be happening in the inn and indeed the village this year. She could not put her finger on it, but something was going to happen. She paused for a few seconds and looked at Henry. 'Are you going to tell them, Henry?'

Henry knew instantly what she was referring to, unlike their guests, who were now left dangling with curiosity. Cynthia insisted that Henry not hold back. Henry thought for a moment and agreed that he would tell them his special story. Before he did so he asked that they listen with open minds to the events that he would relate, events that he believed passionately had happened. He had certainly gained the attention of the Bidders.

Henry began his story.

'My story is about a Christmas tree and some mysterious figures. It is probably the most magical thing ever to have happened to me, other than that is, when I met Myfannwy, and since then I am true believer that Christmas miracles, or at least magical events, do occur.'

Henry paused for a moment and glanced at each of those present.

'When I was ten, I was out playing with my mates Bill and Ben. We were running through the woods at the top of the hill when I stumbled on an old tree stump. The result was a fractured ankle.

What made it worse was that it was a couple of days before Christmas. I ended up spending most of the time in my bedroom here in the inn watching television. Well, on Christmas eve I was laying in my bed. It was quite late, and I was looking out of the bedroom window, feeling sorry for myself, I can tell you.

I was just about to drop off to sleep when I awoke to a noise in the field just outside the window. I got out of bed, hobbled over to the window and there, not more than twenty feet away, were three figures. One was carrying a Christmas tree, one was carrying a shovel, and one was carrying a large box. The one carrying the box seemed to be the one in charge.'

'Who were they, Henry?' asked John.

Henry replied, 'To this very day, John, I do not know.' Joe, having paused his eating to listen to Henry's story asked, 'What happened next?' Henry continued. 'The one with the spade started to dig a hole. After a short time, they planted the tree in it. The tree must have been well over ten feet tall.

There it was, right in front of my bedroom window. In a blinking of an eye that tree was covered with decorations. I remember that they glistened in the moonlight.'

Cynthia suggested that his father had surely arranged it to cheer him up, but Henry responded by saying that although he too first thought that, nobody in fact ever owned up to being there.

'And you are convinced that it was not a dream?' asked Joe.

'Joe, just as sure as you are sitting there, I am one hundred percent positive that it was not a dream. Although I cannot remember every single detail of that evening, I do remember they wore similar clothes and spoke in a language that I did not understand. If Maggie were here, she would probably be saying that they were from Llanelli.'

Henry, as an aside, said he would explain that comment on another occasion. 'That tree remained there until after Christmas. I hobbled out there with my father on Boxing day, but the tree had gone.'

'You mean someone had pinched it.' Joe suggested.

Henry answered, 'When I say the tree had gone, I should have said that the tree had gone, the decorations had gone and,' he paused. 'I have goose bumps just thinking about it. There was no sign of disturbance to the ground whatsoever. Not a single mark.'

Joe suggested that someone had pinched to hole as well, thought better of what he had said, and withdrew his suggestion almost immediately.

'And it has been a mystery ever since.' added Myfannwy.

'There is one thing I do particularly remember.' Henry paused momentarily but continued, 'The one that was giving the orders was nearest to my window. I do recall that he had words written on the front of his top.'

Cynthia suggested that it might have been the name of a company or organisation, but Henry said he did not think so. He was sorry he could not recall anything further and that he could not tell them what the lettering was. Henry went quiet for a moment or two as he was reminiscing the events of that evening but was brought back to the present when Myfannwy spoke.

'If you three just want to laze around during your holiday you are welcome to do so, but I would like to say that we have some wonderful countryside around here to explore and some very entertaining evenings in prospect in these days before Christmas.' Myfannwy smiled as she said this, and Henry added to what his wife had said.

'In addition to the countryside there is the village itself, the village shops and the Church. We do not have a pub, however. As soon as we are able, we will introduce you to Patsy, our vicar. Several of us, and I include Patsy in that number, organise some events in the village. On Wednesday for example we have the elf competition and I know it is an event that you will find very, very entertaining. Every year it turns out to be a barrel of laughs. We just do not know who will turn up, and their costumes, well it is often quite hilarious. Mind you, some take it very seriously.'

'What are the elves competing for Myfannwy?' Cynthia asked.

Myfannwy knew from her tone, and the expressions on the faces of Joe and his father that she had aroused their interest in the elf competition. She explained further. 'We choose a handful of the elves to help Father Christmas on Friday. That is when we have our annual village concert. The local school children sing for us and the elves help our Father Christmas give out presents to the children.'

'How wonderful!' Cynthia exclaimed, 'That sounds like two events we should not miss.' John and Joe voiced their agreement.

CHAPTER NINE

THE ARRIVAL OF THE NORWEGIAN CABBAGE

Meanwhile, outside the building, the Larsens' Volvo was pulling up in the carpark. Asgard, Sofie and Ingrid climbed out of their car and stretched their arms and legs. Sofie was the first to notice that the net, although still securely tied to the roof rack, had lost most of its contents. There was now only one cabbage in it.

'Oh! My dear Asgard,' she exclaimed, 'We have only the one cabbage left!'

Asgard held his head and commented that they had been his 'joy and pride'. He then pointed to the inn. 'I hope Mr. Griffiths has brought many in.' Ingrid asked her parents where they thought the cabbages were now, but her mother suggested that it was best, perhaps, not to know.

Asgard agreed and suggested they unload their cases and make their way indoors, especially as the temperature was dropping. Asgard, aided by Sofie took their cases out of the boot and, with Asgard having retrieved the one remaining cabbage from the top of the car, they made their way to the entrance doors.

Once inside they approached the reception desk, behind which sat Sandra. They put their luggage down but with Asgard retaining possession of the cabbage.

Sandra welcomed them, 'Good evening, you must be the Larsens.'

'Yes, that is true.' Asgard responded. 'We are the Larsens from Norway. God kveld. That means good evening.'

'In that case,' said Sandra, 'god kveld to you and noswaith dda to you. That is good evening to you in Welsh.'

'I shall remember this.' Asgard replied. 'Ah. I see you have a card for me to sign, already.'

Sandra passed Asgard the registration card and as he went to sign it, he passed the cabbage to her over the desk. 'Please excuse the liberty. but could you take control of my cabbage?' Sandra had never been asked that before but took the cabbage off him and placed it to the side.

After he had signed the card he asked. 'May we order some food to be delivered to our rooms? We are all very tired so we would like to retire to our rooms for the night.'

Sandra told them that it was not a problem, said that the menus were in the rooms, and when they were the ready simply to call her on reception. As she was leaving her reception desk to show them to their rooms, she passed Asgard their keys, and assured Asgard that she would take good care of the cabbage. Asgard thanked her and he, Sofie and Ingrid followed her down the corridor.

CHAPTER TEN
THE U.S.A. AND NORWAY UNITE

The following morning, John and Cynthia came down to the dining room for an early breakfast. They were joined by Henry and Myfannwy. Myfannwy commented that they both looked refreshed and suggested that they had recovered from their journey, and that Molly was on duty that morning to serve and take their orders.

'I certainly feel great, Myfannwy,' said Cynthia. 'and John was just saying he too was not suffering at all from any sort of jet lag.'

'Well,' said Henry 'it's a little cold outside but I gather it is going to be a mild day with no rain.'

These four chatted for a while during which time Molly brought in and served their breakfasts.

'What are your plans for today, John?' asked Henry.

It was Cynthia that replied. 'We intend to take a walk to the village this afternoon, and perhaps further afield but, as far as this morning is concerned, we thought we would finish unpacking and then relax in your conservatory.'

'If there's anything that you want just shout.' said Henry. 'Sandra is on reception, but we are always back and fore.' Just as Henry was finishing his sentence, Asgard, Sofie and Ingrid entered the room. 'Ah, you must be the Larsens. Welcome to the Cwtch'

Asgard replied that they were the Larsens and then introduced Sofie and Ingrid. Ingrid was again carrying her camera. Henry, after introducing Myfannwy to them, introduced the Bidders to the Larsens. When the introductions were complete Henry apologised for them not being on hand the previous night to welcome them.

Asgard assured him that was not a problem because they just wanted to, Asgard searched for the right words, and came up with 'hit the pillows.'

Myfannwy invited them to sit at the table and went off to get Molly. 'I will just get Molly and she can take your orders for breakfast.' She was saying this as she left the room.

'That would be nice,' said Sofie.' We are quite hungry.'

'Our son Joseph should be joining us soon. He has accompanied us over to Wales for the holiday.' Cynthia always referred to her son as Joseph. 'He is making it a habit of being late for his meals lately though.'

'And later when Claire can shake herself away from her kitchen, we will introduce you to her.' Henry was saying this at the exact moment that Claire appeared.

'I've given Molly a job to do in the kitchen,' she said, 'so I thought I would take the opportunity to introduce myself and take any further breakfast orders.'

Asgard rose from his chair and shook her hand. 'Hello Claire. I am Asgard Larsen. This is my wife Sofie, and this is my daughter Ingrid.' Claire smiled and said that that she was delighted to meet them. Claire did a quick head count and observed that Joseph was not present, wrote down what everyone wanted, and disappeared back to the kitchen.

Myfannwy returned a few minutes later to the dining room and whispered to Henry that the Larsens seemed to be getting on very well with the Bidders. Henry had made the same observation and said that things had got off to a good start.

'By the way Henry,' she said, 'Claire has left Molly in charge of the kitchen and has popped out to see Patsy about the refreshments and snacks that she wants for the elf evening on Wednesday. I'm going back to help Molly.' Henry nodded and Myfannwy headed off to the kitchen.

Joe appeared at the entrance to the dining room a few minutes later, smiled, and said good morning to everyone. It was Henry that did the honours with the introductions to the Asgard family. Joe then turned to Henry and said, 'I was hoping to put my head around the kitchen door and say hello to Claire. Would that be okay, Henry?'

Henry replied, 'You've just missed her, Joe. She's gone to see the vicar.'

Joe's father commented that they were destined not to meet. They were the proverbial ships in the night.

'Maybe later, then. Can I grab a cup of coffee and waffles? Joe asked.

When Joe had stopped speaking Asgard asked if he could put one quick question to Henry. Henry replied, 'By all means.'

'Are there sufficient cabbages in your stores for the Christmas period?' he asked. 'It was our intention to bring you some home-grown Norwegian King cabbages, but we no longer have them. They have escaped.'

Sofie clarified this. 'What Asgard is trying to say is that we had the cabbages tied to the top of the car, but they must have fallen off somewhere.' Ingrid at this juncture pointed out that there was still one. They had given it to Sandra the previous evening.

'Ah! I see. Rest assured Asgard. We have more than enough.'

'That is good. I am relieved. We have a saying in Norway that a cabbage a day.' He was interrupted by Cynthia saying, 'keeps the doctor away?'

'No. Doctor Johansen is still in the village and visits us occasionally.' Asgard completed what he had started saying. 'The saying is that a cabbage a day makes the brain even more healthy.'

Henry suggested that Joe did visit the kitchen to order up what he wanted and that Molly and Myfannwy were there. A few minutes later he returned with his coffee and a large plate of waffles.

He sat down next to his parents. 'I've just been doing some further research on our Welsh ancestors. There were quite a few Bidders dotted around South Wales. It is going to take some effort to track down any relatives though. Are you coming down to the village with me? I am going down immediately after breakfast.'

His mother informed him that she and his father would be going to the village but in the afternoon. They had been chatting to the Larsens and they were going to spend some time in their company that morning. Sofie added that she had so many questions that she wanted to ask them.

As Joe was eating his waffles, he noticed the camera that was hanging around Ingrid's neck. He asked her if she took many pictures.

'Yes, I do. It is a passion of mine. It is highly efficient Nikon digital camera that my parents bought me last year for my tenth birthday.'

Joe turned to Asgard and asked him what he and his wife did back in Norway. Asgard replied that he was a teacher and proudly, a grower of cabbages. Sofie said that she was a housewife now and helped Asgard with the cabbages on their farm. Joe filled them in with what his family did back in Snow Valley. Having consumed his breakfast Joe bid all farewell and headed out to the village.

CHAPTER ELEVEN
THE CAKE AND MISTAKEN IDENTITY

Joe took his time walking down the half mile or so to the village, stopping every so often to take in what was around him. He stopped for a few minutes at the small bridge that straddled the brook and watched the small fish dart back and fore. He arrived at the end of what he took to be the high street of Pontynant because here were the three shops that Myfannwy had described.

The three shops were next to each in a row and Joe stopped in front of them. He looked and read what was written on the signs above the doors.

The first sign read,
'Pontynant Bakery. Proprietor: Bryn Bacon.'

The second shop sign read,
'Pontynant Butchers. Proprietor: Bill Baker.'

The third sign read,
'Pontynant Post Office. Frank Parcell: Postmaster.'

The bakery shop window was full of different breads and cakes and the butcher's shop had an enormous turkey hanging from a steel bar in its window. A quarter of an hour before Joe arrived at the shops Aggie had entered the cake shop closely followed by Claire. Aggie was ordering a birthday cake for her husband. Claire was standing behind her awaiting her turn.

'Now Bryn,' said Aggie, 'I want that lovely wife of yours to bake my Dougie a birthday cake. It's on the sixth of January remember!'

Bryn who was standing behind his counter wished her a good morning. 'Is it the same theme as last year, Aggie? Star Wars.?'

'Dougie cannot get enough of it.' she replied. 'Now I want a twelve-inch square sponge with white icing on the top and dark icing on the sides. Put a picture of that spacecraft the Aluminium Falcon on the top.'

Bryn then asked her how many layers she wanted to which Aggie replied that she thought there had only ever been one Leia. She went on to say, 'She can go on the top with one Daft Invader and remember that Spanish character, Juan Kenobi.'

'Right,' said Bryn, 'and where would you like Sheila to put the Happy Birthday Dougie?'

'On one of the dark sides, please Bryn.'

'And are you taking him anywhere for his birthday, Aggie?

Aggie replied, 'Wookie Hole as usual.'

'And has he behaved himself enough to go the elf competition?' Bryn asked.

'I suppose so, but I put his good behaviour down to the threat of my death stare if he didn't.'

'I see what you did there, Aggie.'

Aggie was oblivious to what Bryn was referring to but commented. 'He never misses the competition. Never gets selected mind you. Maybe this year. Bye Bryn.'

Aggie turned to leave the shop, noticed Claire, said hello to her, and exited the shop.

Claire stepped up to the counter. It was at this moment that Joe had arrived outside the shops and was digesting the shop signs.

'She never changes, does she?' she suggested to Bryn.

'No, she doesn't. Hello Claire. How are things up at the Cwtch?'

'Very busy at present. Finished after midnight last night. We will get there though. Bryn. Right, I need 4 kilograms of self-raising flour, 2 kilograms of plain and 1 kilogram of rolled oats. Could you deliver it to the Cwtch later?'

Bryn replied that it was not a problem. As he was saying this Joe entered the shop. Claire turned around, glanced at him briefly, and then turned back to Bryn. It was at this point that Joe mistook Claire for his Welsh pistachio lady, Claire's sister Elizabeth.

Joe uttered, 'Oh' It's you and without a Christmas hat this time.'

This clearly made no sense to Claire. 'I'm sorry. Are you speaking to me?' She turned to face him again.

'You do not remember me?' Joe asked.

'No. I don't, but I do recognise an American accent.'

'You did the last time, the last time when you were a bit off with me.' Joe replied.

'Look here, I have never met you before and I am very rarely off with anyone.'

Bryn, believing there could be a scene offered his assistance, but Claire said that everything was okay and that she could cope with his sort. Joe asked that she clarify what she meant by 'his sort'. Claire said that surely he must know the answer to that. He said he did not and that she should enlighten him.

'Unfortunately, I do not have the time. I have things to do.' Claire said.

'Well,' he replied, 'I'm staying at the Cwtch Inn if at any time you want to do that.'

Although Claire had already suspected that Joe was one of the Bidders from America, she had decided not to tell Joe who she was. She did, however, find the things that Joe said confusing. 'You are staying at the Cwtch, eh?' she smiled at Bryn and turned to face Joe again.

'Of course! There is an American family staying there. I had heard that the inn was being invaded. I hope you don't put their backs up like you have mine.'

Joe was quick to reply. 'Look! I did not mean to put your back up, but rest assured I will not be doing that to anyone at the inn. They are nice folks. You could learn a thing or two from the Griffiths family.'

Claire looked at Bryn and smiled again. Bryn smiled back and asked Claire if she wanted to put her purchases on the contra account. She confirmed that she did and that she would arrange to have the items that he wanted to be dropped in later. With that she turned to leave the shop.

Before she did so Joe asked Bryn if he had any pistachios in stock or had this lady snaffled them up again. Claire stopped, looked at him, and said that he was now starting to worry her. She continued to leave the shop but as she did, she said to Joe 'Hywl Fawr.' This is of course goodbye in Welsh but to Joe it sounded that she had just sworn at him. He asked Bryn what it meant. Bryn assured him that it simply meant goodbye. Joe was relieved at that and returned to his question relating to the pistachios.

'Seriously, do you have any pistachios? It's Bryn isn't it?'

'Yes sir, Bryn Bacon at your service. Not to be confused with Bill Baker, the butcher next door. You may also hear people around here call me Bryn the Bread. I am though, one and the same. Bill Baker is better known as Bill the Beef of course, so there should really be no confusion. Now to answer your question. We do indeed have plenty of pistachios. My wife makes a lot of pistachio cheesecakes, you see.'

'Excellent,' replied Joe. 'I will take half a pound.'

'Would you like try one of our Welsh cakes?' Bryn passed Joe one to try. Joe took a bite. 'These are delicious!' he exclaimed. 'I will certainly have half a dozen of those. You don't by chance have the recipe for these, do you?'

Bryn replied. 'I am deeply sorry. Nothing personal, but it's a secret family recipe and I am not allowed to divulge it'

'I can understand that. I am a chef with some secret recipes of my own. Well thank you Bryn, I will see you around. What was that expression? Howell Tha?'

'Close. Hwl Fawr.'

Joe, clutching his bag of pistachios and bag of Welsh cakes, walked out of the shop and back into the street. As he did so he whispered to himself.

'Bryn Bacon the baker a.k.a. Bryn the Bread, Bill Baker the butcher a.k.a. Bill the Beef and a postmaster named Parsell. What is that all about? It must be something Welsh!'

CHAPTER TWELVE
THE OSTRICH

Having exited the cake shop Joe was immediately confronted by the sight of a young schoolboy staring into the butcher's window. Joe guessed that the boy could not be more than nine or ten years old. The boy, with satchel hung over his shoulder was, with mouth wide open, staring at the bird in the window.

'That is a mighty fine specimen, isn't it, kid?' Joe got no response. The boy kept staring at the bird, still open mouthed. 'It's almost your size.' Still there was no response. 'Will you be having a turkey like that for Christmas?' This did bring about a response, but the boy still did not take his eyes of the bird.

'That is not a turkey, mister. It's an ostrich, scientific name Struthio Camelus.'

Joe was somewhat taken back. 'Wow that is impressive, but an ostrich? It is big enough to be an ostrich, but to me it is an exceptionally large turkey. It's too small to be an ostrich surely?'

'My dad said it was an ostrich, and anyway, you can get small ostriches, can't you? A turkey has the scientific name of Meleagris and that is not a meleagris. I collect models of animals.'

'I can't argue with that kid,' Joe replied. 'Here. Take a Welsh cake.' Joe offered him the bag holding the cakes. The boy turned away from the window and took a cake from the bag. As he did so Joe spotted that the boy had a black eye.

'I can see you've been in a fight. That is a real corker of an eye.'

observed Joe.

'For the first time the boy looked directly at Joe. 'Jason Cartwright did it.'

'Did you hit him back?' Joe enquired.

'You're kidding, mister. He is much bigger than me. It would have been murder. My murder!'

Joe offered up a suggestion, 'Look. When I was your age I was bullied in school. One day the bully hit me, but I got the courage up and hit him back. He kept his distance after that. You should try it.'

The boy did not say anything to Joe's suggestion and turned to look at the bird again.

'Are you going to buy the ostrich?' he asked Joe.

'No. I don't think so.' Joe replied.

'Anyway, I have to go now. Diolch. Thank you for the Welsh cake.' With that the boy started to walk away.

'You're welcome.' Joe replied.

Joe watched him walk up the street for a few moments and whispered words of assurance to himself that the bird in the window was indeed a turkey. No sooner had he said this to himself than the boy, who must have been at least thirty yards away, turned, and shouted to Joe, 'It's an ostrich, I tell you!'

Joe shouted back. 'Okay kid. Have a great day!'

CHAPTER THIRTEEN
THE U.S.A. MEETS MAGGIE

Joe did wonder whether the boy would be alright and whether he, himself, should tell someone. Perhaps they already knew. He did not have any further time to dwell on this however, because the morning was going to get even more interesting for him. As he started to turn, he almost walked into an old lady who had crept up quietly behind him. It was Maggie.

'Good morning. You startled me there for a moment.' He said taking a step backwards.

'I've been told I do that a lot.' said Maggie. 'I have been told it is hereditary. My mother used to frighten people and cats. Still does in fact.' She looked Joe up and down. 'Haven't seen you in the village before, my darling.'

Joe replied, 'No. First time in Ponteenant. Is that how you pronounce it?'

'Good enough. I have heard it spoken worse. I have said it worserer myself. Where are you from then? You are not from Llanelli, are you? I don't like people from Llanelli!'

Joe asked her why she did not like anyone from this place called Llanelli. She replied that it was because her husband had come from there.

'That's why!' she proclaimed. 'What other reason do you need?'

Joe feeling slightly uncomfortable, ventured to say that he was not from Llanelli. 'Don't worry I am not from there. I am from the United States.'

'Where's that then?' enquired Maggie.

'Oh! It's a long way from here.'

'Further than Llanelli?'

'Oh yes. Much further. My home is situated the other side of the big pond.'

'Near to farmer Myles' land then? He lives on the other side of the pond.'

'No, no. It's a different pond.' Joe confirmed.

Maggie looked puzzled. 'I didn't know there was another pond. I will have to keep a look out for that one, boyo.' She paused for a moment and then glanced up at the window. 'By the way, his name was Buddy.' Joe looked up the street to see if he could still see the boy.

'He seemed a nice enough kid.' Joe commented believing that she was talking about the boy.

'Not the boy! The boy's name is Jeremy. I was talking about the turkey hanging up there.' She pointed to the turkey.' I know his name was Buddy because I grew it. Bill the Beef is taking it up to the Cwtch later. They are having it for Christmas dinner, isn't it? It is the only place around here with an oven big enough, you see. I have got an invite you know. I get one every year since my husband passed away.'

Joe was trying to get his head around the fact that she had

called the turkey Buddy but managed to tell her that he was in fact staying at the Cwtch over the Christmas period.

'I'll be there as well.' She pointed again at the turkey. 'I called him Buddy after my dog.'

'Ah! You have a dog then?' asked Joe.

'Well. I do not have a dog, but if I did, I would call him Buddy.'

Rather hesitantly Joe commented., 'It's certainly a fine specimen.'

She replied, 'It should be boyo. I fed him on the best food. Carrots, crisps, potatoes, boiled eggs, cheese and cream crackers. But I am relying on you not telling anyone, right? I also fed him Brussel sprouts.'

Joe could only say, 'You don't say!'

Maggie replied. 'Well, I did just say. He was a noisy old sod though. Wouldn't stop singing.'

'Singing?' Joe needed clarification on that.

'See. That is why I know you are not from around here. I thought with your accent you might have been from Newcastle, but now that you have questioned the singing you are definitely not from around here, isn't it? What you pond people must appreciate is that he was Welsh. He sang twenty-five hours a day and all through the night. That is not me saying that he sang the song All Through the Night, you understand. That would be ridiculous!'

Joe nodded his head in agreement. Maggie continued. 'He would keep the neighbours awake. Well, he would have kept the neighbours awake if I had any neighbours that is. Goodness knows what would have happened if I had raised several of the little devils. Most likely they would have formed a choir, isn't it?'

'That would have been a nightmare for sure!' commented Joe.

'Buddy had much in common with my mother, you see.'

Joe questioned whether this was the singing that they had in common.

'No boyo. The looks.'

Joe was asking himself at this point whether to beat a hasty retreat, but Maggie pulled on his sleeve. She had not finished with him yet.

'It was a hell of a task plucking it' she said.' Would not stop running around the yard. Anyway, I cannot let you keep me talking like this. I had better be off. I've got things to do.' She paused for a second. 'I think! I will keep an eye out for that other pond. Have a safe trip home but avoid Llanelli, isn't it?

Joe drew breath and said he would see her around. Maggie then scurried off up the street.

CHAPTER FOURTEEN
JOE MEETS PATSY

Joe watched Maggie as she scurried away and paused where he was for a moment to fully absorb and take in all the imagery that had just been presented to him. As he was in this world of contemplation, Patsy, the local vicar appeared next to him. She was struggling carrying a large cardboard box.

'Penny for your thoughts,' she said. 'on this wonderful Monday morning.'

'Yes. Good morning to you. Hey, that looks heavy. Can I help you with that?'

'Please. That would be great. I had forgotten how heavy these decorations are.'

Joe noticed the dog collar that Patsy was wearing. 'I am assuming that from the dog collar you are the local vicar.' Joe took the box off Patsy and they started to walk.

'That is correct, and I am assuming, from that accent and your age that you must be Joseph Bidder. Claire has told me all about the guests at the inn this Christmas.'

'Where are you heading to with these, Reverend?'

'Patsy, please. Just to the village hall over there.' She pointed to the building in question. It was about forty yards further up the street and just off to the side. 'We are in the process of decorating the hall for this week's events.'

'Yes, Henry has been telling us about the plans.'

'I couldn't help noticing that you were talking to Maggie.'

'That was Maggie was it. She's an interesting character, isn't she?'

As they continued their chat Maggie walked towards them and as she was passing said, 'Morning, Vicar. I was going in the wrong direction, isn't it? Do not worry, vicar! He is not from Llanelli. He's a pond person apparently, but it's not Farmer Myles' pond you understand.' Maggie passed them and when she had gone Patsy asked Joe if he understood what she had meant by the expression 'pond person'. Joe duly explained.

'She has this hang up over people from Llanelli and we have all come to accept that as the norm.' Patsy commented. 'She is a little scatty and eccentric but she's harmless. I will say, however, she is in the church every Sunday, without fail, belting out the hymns and I mean belting them out.'

'Just like her ostrich, then? I mean her turkey, Buddy?'

Patsy chuckled. 'She told you about her turkey, then? Maggie lives on the edge of the village. Her husband passed away a few years ago. Do you know? Other than a couple of trips to Cardiff to visit her mother in the care home, I don't think she has ever left the village.'

'So. She's a little eccentric then? Joe asked.

'Her husband, Cyril, was just the same. They were well suited that is for sure! Last Christmas it was Maggie that spread the news around the village that there had been a murder in the village hall.'

'What?' asked Joe, somewhat surprised.'A murder?'

'Actually Joseph.' Patsy was interrupted by Joe.

'Please, call me Joe.'

'Well Joe. There was not a murder. Maggie was in the village hall when the Christmas tree fell on one of the parishioners. Maggie went around telling everyone that old Mr. Cole had been stabbed a hundred times. In fact, he had only suffered puncture marks from the tree's needles. Maggie has always maintained that the Christmas tree was out to get her and fell on old Ken Cole by mistake.'

'It makes life interesting doesn't it, Patsy? At least most of your flock thus far seem friendly.'

'Most?' questioned Patsy. 'Why only most?'

'I think I just upset one of them. I upset her yesterday and then again this morning in the shop.'

'And who was that then, Joe?'

'I didn't get her name.'

'Don't go upsetting too many of my congregation, Joe.'

'I've come over with my parents for a couple of weeks. It is a complete break from our business in the States. I was a little hesitant about agreeing to come, but with Dad having Welsh ancestry and with him insisting that we visit the place of our roots what could I do? However, I must say that other than the Pistachio Lady I am rather enjoying it here.'

'Pistachio lady? What is that all about?' asked Patsy.

'That's the young lady that I fell out with. It is a long story. I won't bore you.'

They arrived at the village hall at the same time as Maggie was passing them again but in the opposite direction to before. Maggie pointed down the street and said, 'It was this way after all.'

As she passed, Patsy said to her, 'See you in church, Maggie.' She then turned to Joe and thanked him for his help. She took the box off him and said that there should be plenty of people inside to help her from here. Once today's tasks were completed all that was left was the collection of the Christmas tree from the farm in the morning.

Joe offered his help in that regard. Patsy replied that he was exceedingly kind, and she would take him up on his offer, so they duly planned to meet up at the inn early the following morning. Patsy disappeared into the hall and Joe embarked upon his return walk to the inn.

CHAPTER FIFTEEN
MISTAKEN IDENTITY CONTINUED

Had Joe entered the village hall with Patsy he would have discovered Claire was one of the people helping Patsy prepare the village hall for the elf competition on the Wednesday and the carol concert on the Friday. Perhaps then Joe would have found out who the lady in the cake shop was, but it was not yet to be. Claire, who had entrusted her kitchen to Molly and her parents, knew that she would be in the village hall well into the afternoon.

There was a group of ten people busily, cleaning, sorting furniture and chairs and putting up decorations. They were of course leaving space for the Christmas tree.

One conversation that did take place in the hall that afternoon, and over a well-deserved cup of tea, was that between Claire and Patsy. Patsy was keen to tell Claire that she had met the young American from the inn that morning and when Claire mentioned that she had met him in the cake shop earlier, and they had not exactly seen eye to eye, it dawned on Patsy who Joe was referring to as the Welsh pistachio lady.

However, what Joe had said to Claire in their conversation still did not make sense to either Claire or Patsy. What was the pistachio business all about? What was it about the Christmas hat that Claire was not wearing?

Claire and Patsy both agreed that Joe was a good looking individual but perhaps, as Patsy put it, 'He was a cent short of a dollar.'

One thing in his favour, from Claire's point of view, was that Joe had been quick to say that her parents were 'nice folks'.

Exhausted from her endeavours in the village hall, Claire had returned to the inn at tea-time but after chatting to her parents for a short while retired to her room for a nap. She was half expecting to bump into Joe at some point but Joe, on his return from the village that morning, had spent some time lounging in the conservatory and chatting to the Larsens as well as playing with Bonnie.

When his parents returned mid-afternoon, he stayed with them for a while but then informed that he was going to his room to do some serious family research on his computer.

Henry and Myfannwy let Claire sleep on into the evening. They and Molly took care of the kitchen and the evening meals for the guests. Joe, now deeply entrenched in his searches, had a meal delivered to his room.

Claire awoke from her slumber and decided, that even though it was nine o'clock she would make her way to the kitchen to aid in any way she could.

Joe, meanwhile, had looked at the clock, which told him it was ten o'clock, and decided that he had done enough for the evening. He closed his computer and made his way to the lounge for a drink. Kenneth was on hand to oblige. He joined his parents and the Larsens in conversation for the next half an hour or so.

By eleven o'clock the only person left in the lounge was Joe, but he did have the company of Bonnie. At the same time the only person left in the kitchen was Claire who was giving the surfaces a good clean before she shut the kitchen for the night.

Once she had completed this task she exited the kitchen and locked the kitchen door. She began to walk down the corridor towards the lounge but, as she drew nearer, she could hear a voice. It was Joe talking to Bonnie. She stopped at the lounge doorway but held back to eavesdrop. Joe was speaking quietly to Bonnie at this point.

'You're a friendly soul aren't you girl? Most around here are to be fair. I did have a run in with one pretty young lady down in the cake shop this morning.' He paused for a second. 'The Welsh pistachio lady.'

Claire entered the lounge and stood in front of him. Bonnie made a fuss of her. Are you talking about me?' she asked. Joe was taken back by her sudden entrance and jumped up.'

'I guess so.' he replied.

'Welsh pistachio lady! What is that all abought, for goodness sake?' She raised her voice slightly but not enough to wake anyone.

'I didn't realise that there was anyone else around.' whispered Joe. 'Henry said that my family and the Norwegian family were the only guests in the inn.'

'And he would be right. I'm Claire.'

'Claire. The Chef? Henry's daughter.'

'Correct on both counts.'

'Look. I think we have got off on the wrong foot. I am Joe, Joe Bidder. I will not mention the pistachio incident again, so shall we start again? What do you say?' The pistachio business still puzzled Claire but she responded positively to his request.

'I don't understand half of what you are saying, but it is Christmas, and you are a guest of the inn so yes, okay.'

'That's great!' replied Joe.

There was a moment of silence between them, an awkwardness only broken by them saying goodnight to each other at the same time. Joe was now aware that the lady in the cake shop was Claire, but still believed that she and the person he met on the train were one and the same.

He was in for a big surprise a few days later. They went off in different directions to their respective rooms for the night, both wondering what the next day would bring.

CHAPTER SIXTEEN
TREE HUNTING PLANS

It was Tuesday morning and all the Cwtch's guests were down in the dining room for early breakfasts. Henry was coming out of the dining room as Myfannwy arrived at the dining room doors, having come from the reception.

'All our guests are down having breakfast, Myfannwy, and getting on with each other splendidly.' He glanced back into the dining room and continued. 'There's that lovely Christmas atmosphere here again, don't you think?' he asked.

'I totally agree, Henry, and I still have that feeling in my bones that something wonderful is going to happen. Look, I am popping down to see Claire about tonight's meal arrangements. Before I do, dare I mention Sammy the Skip?'

'All in hand my dear. He promised he would be here tomorrow afternoon. By the way did I mention that one of John's ancestors was a boxer?'

'Yes, you did.' Myfannwy was walking away from him but turned back. 'We'll have to make special arrangements tomorrow regarding the meals because of the elf evening.' She paused for a moment. 'Henry, I was with Claire early this morning and.'

'And what?' Henry asked.

'Well, she seems to have an extra sparkle about her.'

'Can't say I have noticed.'

'Why doesn't that surprise me? Anyway, I am off to see Claire. I'll catch up with you in a moment or two.' She headed off to the kitchen and Henry headed towards reception to make a further call to Sammy the Skip.

Within ten minutes, Henry and Myfannwy were back in the dining room and chatting to John and Asgard, whilst Cynthia and Sofie were at the other end of the table talking about their respective families. Joe, with Claire close in attendance, was discussing Ingrid's camera which she had been carrying for much of the time she had been at the Cwtch.

Joe turned to Claire, smiled and complimented on the cooked breakfast that he had just consumed. Myfannwy came over to join them. 'You've certainly impressed Joe with your cooking, Claire.'

Claire smiled at her mother. 'Thank you, mother. I do my best.' Claire then asked all at the table what they were going to do today.

Sofie was the first to reply. 'Asgard, Ingrid and I are going down to the village again.'

'Yes.' Said Asgard. 'We have the bibs and bobs still to buy.' He turned to face Myfannwy. 'Now you are sure I cannot get you any more cabbages. Myfannwy? It would be of no trouble.'

'Rest assured, Asgard.' she replied. 'We have plenty.'

At this point Cynthia asked if she and John could join them in their walk. Sofie said that would be wonderful if they did join them.

'What are you up to, Joe?' asked Myfannwy.

'I am meeting up with Patsy.' He replied.

'The Vicar?' asked Claire. 'And on first name terms already? Be careful Joe. Patsy is on the lookout for a husband at present.'

'We are going to get a tree for the village hall. That is all! I met her yesterday in the village.'

'Yes, I know.' Said Claire. 'She told me all about it.'

'She did, did she?' Joe smiled. 'I am going to be careful what I say in future. Seems things get around this village like wildfire. Like Maggie with her murder.' With Joe having said that last statement Henry had to explain to the others what that was all about.

Ingrid, looking hopefully, asked her mother whether she could go tree hunting with Joe instead of going to the village with her parents. The answer was yes but she had to get properly dressed for the job and if it was okay with Joe. Ingrid looked at Joe and smiled widely.

'Joe?' she asked.

'Fine by me kiddo. I have got to get changed as well so why don't we meet up in reception in say, ten minutes? Patsy should be here by then.'

Ingrid went off to her room to get changed. Claire sat down next to Joe and suggested that someone seemed to have a crush on him. He asked if she meant Patsy, but Claire told him it was Ingrid that she was referring to. Myfannwy was at that precise moment standing by Henry in the doorway.

In a whisper, she said to her husband. 'You know what Henry. I get the distinct impression that the sparkle I told you about earlier is to do with Joe.' Myfannwy could see that she was not getting through to him. 'Henry, they like each other!'

'But they've only just met.' replied Henry.

'It was the same with us, Henry. Don't you remember, dear?' Myfannwy looked at her husband wondering if he would recall their early days.

Henry said he did, but Myfannwy knew he was struggling to remember so she changed the subject to that of their other daughter, Elizabeth.

CHAPTER SEVENTEEN
THE SEARCH FOR THE NORDMAN BEGINS

Joe, having changed into more suitable clothing, walked to reception. There was no sign of Ingrid, so he chatted to Sandra. He asked her how she was this day and Sandra replied that she was fine.

'May I enquire as to where you are off to today, Joe?' she asked.

'Ingrid and I are hooking up with Patsy, the vicar, and we are off to find a tree for the village hall.'

'Patsy, eh? You know she's looking for a husband?'

'So, I have been informed.' Joe changed the subject. Whilst he thought Patsy a lovely person that is as far as it went. 'Are you working the Christmas?'

'I am indeed. I don't mind though.'

'At least you are taking Ingrid with you for protection against the vicar.'

'Rest assured. I can protect myself.'

At this moment Ingrid joined them. She was carrying her camera. Joe asked her if she was ready to go. She replied that she just wanted to take some photos of the inflatables in the hall, and she would be ready. Joe therefore continued chatting to Sandra during which the subject of the elf competition arose.

'Are you entering the elf competition tomorrow night? 'Sandra asked.

'No chance!' Joe quickly replied. 'It's not for me!'

'You are going to it though?'

'We all are. We've been told it is a very entertaining evening.'

'It certainly is. I am working tomorrow night, unfortunately but, by the look of it, I will be able to see the photographs.' She pointed to Ingrid who was now returning to them. Joe felt a tug on his jacket sleeve.

'Come on Joe.' she said. 'I'm ready.'

'Let us go then.' Joe looked at Sandra, 'I've been summoned. See you later Sandra.'

Joe and Ingrid made their way to the front doors and then out into the carpark. They met Patsy who had that moment arrived and Joe introduced Ingrid to Patsy. Patsy and Joe walked side by side up the drive, across a small enclosure, and through a side gate to the lane that would lead them to the farm that was selling the Christmas trees. Ingrid, who was snapping away with her camera, was walking close behind.

'So, Patsy. What size tree are you after?' Joe asked.

Patsy replied that it had to be no more than eight feet in height.

'You should get a Nordman Fir,' commented Ingrid. 'Trust me! I am from Norway.'

'Okay Ingrid. A Nordman it shall be.' Patsy replied. 'and I

think you should decide which particular tree which we shall have.'

'Thank you,' said Ingrid, 'I shall pick a good one.'

Joe stopped and turning to Patsy asked, 'What's this with the elf competition? I have heard different people talk about it. It sounds like it's quite a boisterous occassion'

Patsy laughed. 'That's one way to describe it. My predecessor, who first organised the concert, thought it would be a good idea to add a visit from Father Christmas to give out presents to the local school children. Several local villagers took it upon themselves to dress up as elves to help Father Christmas.

Since then, we have held an elf competition to choose the five or six we need. Normally it is friendly rivalry between the hopefuls but last year it escalated into a bit of a farce, well a bit of a punch up if I am to be truthful.'

'What, the children got out of hand?'

'No, not the children. It was the elves, the adults. You had to be there to believe it.'

'I think I will definately be an observer then.'

Ingrid, who had continued to take photographs, but who had also been listening to the conversation between Joe and Patsy, had a question about the elves.

'Pardon me, but what is this elf that you are talking about?' Patsy replied that it was a sort of character from folklore and that nowadays they are associated with helping Father Christmas. 'Now I know this. In Norway, we call them Elleve. They are the same for sure. We also have barn gnomes. They are not as nice.'

Joe enquired of Ingrid as to how Christmas was celebrated in Norway. Ingrid replied. 'It varies. In my home we celebrate mostly on the eve of Christmas. We exchange presents then.

After Christmas day we visit family and friends and eat a lot and eat a lot more.' Patsy asked what type of food they had. 'For sure, we have turkey on Christmas Day, but my favourite foods are on the Eve when we have ribbe, that is ribs of pork and lutefisk, that is cured cod. Of course, in my home we eat a lot of cabbage.'

On hearing this Joe smiled and chuckled. 'I know what you are thinking, Joe. Perhaps with all that cabbage we suffer with the hastighetts. I think the English word for this is ...'

Patsy interrupted, 'I think you mean wind?'

Ingrid laughed. 'I was thinking of another word, but wind is good. For some reason, our family does not suffer from the hastighetts,' she paused momentarily. 'the winding.'

'And do you have Christmas Pudding?' Patsy asked.

'We do not have the pudding that you eat. My favourite is ris pudding. It is a hot rice pudding.' Joe asked whether that was with cabbage.

Ingrid smiled. 'No, Joe. That would be silly, wouldn't it?'

Patsy agreed and they continued their walk.

CHAPTER EIGHTEEN
THE LAW CATCHES UP WITH MAGGIE

Whilst the three intrepid tree hunters continued their quest, P.C. Thorncroft, the local police officer, was on his beat around the village. He was particularly on the look-out for Maggie. His luck was in for who should come out of the post office right next to him was the lady in question.

'Ah! Maggie. The very person I wanted to speak to.'

'I haven't done anything wrong officer Thorncroft, have I?'

'You know what you've been doing, Maggie. You have been writing 'But not if you are from Llanelli' on our village welcome sign.'

'How do you know it was me then? You've got fingerprints, have you?'

'Maggie, you signed it!'

'Oh.' She started to shuffle on the spot.

'And did you have anything to do with those two cabbages that I found by the sign?'

'Nothing to do with me that is, isn't it? They were there when I got there. Thought best leave them there, I did.'

'You've gone too far this time, Maggie.'

'That's unfair. I only walked to the end of the village, honest!'

'I did not mean that! I meant that you have done something again that you should not have. This is the third time this month that I have had to speak to you. First was because I received that complaint from Mrs. Carmichael over her traumatised cat, and the second was when your turkey, Buddy, escaped and I had a traumatised Mrs. Carmichael on my hands.'

'She shouldn't have shouted at him. He did not like anyone shouting at him. He was a sensitive soul, isn't it?'

'Tell me, Maggie. Why do you not like people from Llanelli? It can't just be because of Cyril.'

'He was not the only reason, that's true. Look, when Cyril and I got married it was here in the local church. The vicar before Patsy, Reverend Windon, performed the ceremony. I would have asked Patsy, but she was not here then, you see. Anyways, Cyril's family from Llanelli were all invited to come here, so they hired a bus. On the way, someone had the bright idea to stop off to get some fish and chips. That church smelt of salt and vinegar something awful.'

'Oh dear, Maggie. That is bad!'

'But it got worse, officer Thorncroft. Some had faggots and peas and Cyril could not resist a good faggot and peas. He spent all the ceremony with a piece of faggot and two peas stuck to the top of his carnation.' She paused to take breath.

'They all drank like fish as well.'

'Everyone likes a good a drink at a wedding, Maggie.'

'But this was in the church! We could hardly hear the vicar speak over the clanking of bottles and glasses.'

'Surely the vicar said something?'

'He did say something. I heard him say, 'Dear Lord, please ensure that I get through this day, unscathed, and soon'!'

'Did they dress for the occasion though?'

'Don't make me laugh! You have never seen as many boiler suits, jeans, tee shirts, hoodies, and flip flops in your life. I think what capped it off though were their buttonholes.'

'I gather there was something wrong with the flowers?'

'Flowers? They turned up with rosettes pinned to their tops, rosettes that they had borrowed from the Llanelli and Area District Pony Club. Just in their first row in the church they had one first, two seconds and one best turned-out pony.'

'But surely, Maggie. You family did do something about them?'

'None of my family turned up! They were too scared to, isn't it?'

'Go on your way, Maggie, and no more graffiti!' They went their separate ways.

CHAPTER NINETEEN
THE NORDMAN FIR IS FOUND

After about half a mile, Joe with Patsy and Ingrid arm in arm, arrived at the farmgate of Court Farm. Just inside the gate they found Jim, the owner, and fifty or so cut Christmas trees of different types and sizes. Jim stopped trimming one of the trees to talk to his visitors.

'Hello vicar. Who do we have here then?'

'Good morning James. This is Joe from America and this is Ingrid from Norway.'

'Bore da, to you both. America and Norway, you say. I'm assuming that you are guests staying at the Cwtch.'

'That's right. We're staying over the Christmas holidays.' Joe shook Jim's hand.

'I was up at the Cwtch the other day and Myfannwy told me all about you.'

Ingrid put her hand out and Jim shook it. 'We are looking for an eight-foot Nordman Fir, if you have one, please.'

Patsy added that Ingrid was their expert adviser as far as the choice of tree was concerned.

'A good choice I must say. The problem is that I do not have any left in the yard. Sold the last one yesterday. However, I do have Nordmans up in the upper fields. You are very welcome to go up there and find one.'

'We will do that, James. By the way I didn't see you in church last Sunday.' Patsy knew that it was because Jim was always extremely busy at this time of year.

'I'll tell you what I am going to do, Patsy. If I let you have the tree for free you must forgive me for my absence. Do we have a deal?'

Patsy turned to Ingrid. 'What do you think, Ingrid?'

'My thought is that it is a good arrangement. Yes Joe,?'

Joe agreed, was given a saw by James for the task in hand, and the three left James looking for another saw to continue his work. They returned to the lane and started up the last section of the lane towards the woodland area that Jim grew his trees in.

A few minutes later the three climbed over a wooden style, crossed a small field and found themselves in a small clearing in the woods. Around them were growing Christmas trees. Joe and Patsy sat down together on a patch of ground. Patsy took a photograph of them amidst the surrounding Christmas trees.

She was however keen to make a start hunting for the Nordman fir.

'Whilst you two oldies catch your breath.' She smiled. 'May I go and search for our tree?'

'Not so much of the oldies, young lady.' replied Patsy. 'I have to admit though a five-minute sit down would be nice. What about you, Joe?'

Joe replied that he too would welcome a short rest before the rigours of cutting a tree down. They allowed Ingrid to start searching if she did not go far. In an instant she had disappeared.

Joe started to look around at his surroundings. 'You know what Patsy. The more I look around, and the more I take in the smell of these trees, the more it reminds me of Snow Valley. Every year we go out as a family to cut down the family's Christmas tree.'

Patsy was also taking in the surroundings. 'I come up here a lot. I can relax up here and get divine inspiration for my sermons. I have been here four years now and I am still discovering places up here. I'm hoping that the authorities see fit to keep me here for a long time yet.'

'You seem quite happy here.' Joe commented. 'It must be more than just busy for you at this particular time of year, with church affairs and all these extra events that you are involved with. You are very much like Claire in that your both hard workers.'

'Claire works hard for sure. She's a lovely young lady.' Patsy looked enquiringly at Joe to see his reaction to her comment.

'I think we are on speaking terms now but at first I think she took a disliking to me. That was the young lady that I had the disagreement with over a packet of pistachios, would you believe?' He paused for a moment and then asked, 'Pasty, please excuse me for asking this question but does Claire have a memory problem?'

'Why? Patsy enquired.

'Well. She does not seem to recall the pistachio incident and it also drew a blank when I mentioned the Christmas hat.'

'She has never come over as having a problem with her memory, Joe. Perhaps it is due to all the work she is doing.'

'That's probably it.'

'I know she thinks you're cute, a little strange but cute, nevertheless. I talked to her on the phone this morning just before I came out to meet you.'

'Cute? I do not want to be cute. Come to think of it I don't to be regarded as strange either.'

Patsy thought it best at this point to change the subject. 'I understand your folks own a restaurant back home?'

'That's right. It is doing well now. I spoke to my uncle Luigi last night. They seem to be managing without us and to be honest I am really enjoying being here in Wales for the holidays. I'm here with my parents visiting the country of my father's ancestors.'

'Talking about the events we are holding this year will you be participating in our elf competition. I can always wrestle up a costume for you.'

'I am going to be there as a spectator.' Joe was insistent that would be the case.

'Claire and I are two of the judges in tomorrow night's elf competition. Henry has enlisted a special guest to be a third judge but only he knows who it is.' She paused for a moment. 'I meant to ask you, how are the Larsens? Ingrid seems a nice girl.'

'The Larsens are okay. They want to join in everything just like mum and dad. We all seem to be getting on well together, but I am a little perplexed by this desire they have, to eat so many cabbages.' Joe realised that they had been sitting for a while. 'Hey! We'd better find out where Ingrid has got to.' Just as he finished talking however, Ingrid appeared. She had been running and was out of breath.

'Come on you two, I have found our tree!' She exclaimed. 'Come quickly!'

Joe and Patsy rose to their feet and followed Ingrid out of the clearing.

CHAPTER TWENTY
WAS IT THE SQUIRREL?

After they had jogged a hundred or so yards, they came to a smaller, second clearing. Patsy, Joe and Ingrid arrived at the tree that Ingrid had discovered. Joe and Patsy inspected it and agreed that it was the perfect tree for the hall.

'How do you say perfect in Norwegian, Ingrid?' Patsy asked.

'Perfekt.' was her reply. 'Before we do anything else could I ask you a question, Patsy? Do your elves live in the woods?' Patsy replied that it was possible that they could live anywhere. 'I think then that we have elves in these woods.'.

Joe was about to ask why she had asked this, but before he could, there was the sound of a muffled, what Ingrid would call, a hastighett.

There was a moment's silence and then a voice was heard coming from behind one of the nearby trees. 'Sergeant. Was that one of our men that hoofed?'

Another voice, from behind another tree, replied. 'Must have been a squirrel sir.'

'Sergeant, since when has a squirrel tried to hide a hoof?'

'I've not known it in my lifetime, major.'

'Well then sergeant?'

'It was Private Hornby, sir.'

Private Hornby thought it best at this juncture to own up.

'Sorry Major.'

The sergeant appropriately commented that it had blown their cover somewhat. All the time Patsy, Joe and Ingrid had been listening to the conversation but, as yet, they had not seen the people behind those voices. The major spoke again. 'Hornby should know well enough now Sergeant not to allow any noise to be expelled whilst undertaking anti detection manoeuvres.'

'Indeed sir.'

'Well sergeant as you have so eloquently put it, Hornby has blown our cover, so get your men assembled immediately in this clearing.' There was rustling in the trees and out stepped a Territorial Army Major, his sergeant and four privates. They were all wearing camouflage and had blackened faces. The major approached Patsy, Ingrid and Joe and saluted.

'Good morning. I am Major Timothy Sunderland-Brown of the Territorial Army. I do apologise for disturbing you. Ah I see you are a woman of the cloth. Double apologies.' He looked at the saw that Joe was carrying. 'Getting a tree for Christmas, eh? It is so refreshing to see a family out together on such a quest.'

Joe was the first to reply. 'We're not related Major. The Reverend here is from the village and Ingrid and I are guests at the Cwtch Inn.'

Ingrid, looking at the army personnel, commented. 'We thought you were elves.'

The major replied with a chuckle. 'Elves, you say. This bunch would probably do better if they were elves. Is that a Norwegian accent?' Ingrid replied that it was. 'I thought so. Spent a year just outside Oslo. Lovely place.' The major attempted to say Merry Christmas but came out with God Bagatelle which, when translated, meant merry trifle. Ingrid looked at him and just smiled.

Joe asked the major whether they were on long term manoeuvres, to which the major replied. 'We certainly are. The men are learning about camouflage, stealth and evasion.' He turned to his sergeant at that moment. 'I believe we need to repeat the training, sergeant.'

'I will organise that sir.'

Ingrid asked the major if she could take a photograph of his men but the major replied that it was against the rules. He apologised but offered to take one of her with Patsy and Joe.

Ingrid passed him the camera, the major took the photograph, and handed Ingrid back the camera. As he was doing this. he turned to his sergeant. 'Before you do anything else Sergeant, I want you to get the men to cut down that fine specimen of a tree and transport it down the hill to wherever the Reverend requires.' The sergeant jumped into action, saluted his officer, and organised his men accordingly.

Patsy thanked him and added. 'If they could take it down the hill to the village hall that would be good of them. You and your men are welcome to join us at any of our events this week, Major. We have the elf judging competition in the village hall tomorrow and there is a carol concert there on Friday. There will hot soup and snacks tomorrow night.'

The major's face lit up on hearing this. 'My men and I are here until Thursday night. Tomorrow night we are on night vision training up in the woods so we may just pop in to have some of that hot soup. It's pretty cold up here in the woods at night, but my men are a pretty resilient bunch.' At that very instant one of his men sneezed. 'Who was that Sergeant?'

'It was Pincott, sir. Says that the rain we had earlier went down his neck.'

The major looked at Patsy, gave a wry smile, and asked her if she had any spare elves to replace the numpties that he had. The sergeant added to the major's frustration. 'I do have a request from one of the other men, sir. Private Lawson wants to know whether we could do the night vision training tomorrow afternoon instead of tomorrow night. He's got a bowls match tomorrow evening.'

The major smiled again at Patsy. 'And this was the best of the bunch, would you believe?' He then saluted our three Christmas tree hunters and as he was about to turn Ingrid thanked him.

'Takk Major'

This the major did understand but his reply was again a little way off being correct, indeed a little way off making sense. 'Kryss Tokk, young lady.' He did not know that this just meant tick tock. Ingrid was too polite to correct him, and the others were blissfully ignorant.

CHAPTER TWENTY-ONE
THE PIANIST

By the time Joe and Ingrid got back to the inn it was lunchtime. Joe's parents and Ingrid's parents had gone for a walk and a shopping trip and had not yet returned. Bob and Gregor were busy working in the workshop on the sleigh for the Friday. Henry and Myfannwy were in the office doing paperwork and Molly and Claire were in the kitchen. Joe and Ingrid had lunch with Claire and, when they had finished, they retreated to the lounge to relax.

'So! The Christmas tree is in the village hall. I bet Patsy is relieved.' said Claire as she sat close to Joe on the settee and Ingrid sat in the chair by the fire.

'We had the help of Major Tikk Tokk, so we ended up really just having a good walk ourselves.'

'Major Tikk Tokk?' asked Claire with a puzzled look on her face.

'That is what Joe and I have decided to call him, Claire. We are calling his men the little squirrels'. Claire looked even more puzzled, but Joe explained to her the full events of the morning. This led them to look at each other and say together. 'Hastigettes' and laughing out loud. It was at this precise moment that Myfannwy entered the lounge accompanied by Bonnie, who after making a fuss of Ingrid, jumped onto the settee and nestled in between Claire and Joe.

'Bonnie and I are having a break from the paperwork.' Myfannwy commented as she sat in one of the other chairs by the fire. 'How did it go with the tree this morning?'

Joe answered that the mission had been carried out successfully and by now the tree should be standing proudly in the village hall. Ingrid added that they managed to find a beautiful Nordman fir. Myfannwy noticed that Ingrid was not carrying her camera and asked her where it was. Ingrid replied that it was taking a rest. Myfannwy called Bonnie off the settee and Claire took the opportunity to move closer to Joe.

'You two seem to be getting on well.' Myfanwy observed as she looked towards Joe and her daughter.

'We seem to have a lot in common it seems.' Claire replied. 'We do have our own special and well-guarded recipes for example.'

'And it seems like it's going to stay that way.' added Joe.

'I suppose,' Claire paused. 'I suppose as we will soon be three thousand miles apart it wouldn't be a problem if we shared some of our secrets.'

'There you go.' Said Myfannwy. 'A step forward.'

Joe agreed and went on to say. 'I would really love to get hold of Bryn the Bread's Welsh cake recipe.' At this point Claire and her mother looked at each other and started to laugh. 'Okay. What is so funny?' he asked.

Myfannwy looked at Claire to seek approval to tell Joe. Claire nodded her head.

'Joe. Bryn buys his Welsh cakes from Claire. It is her special recipe. Bryn just doesn't let on who makes them.'

'In that case Claire, can I have the recipe? I promise not to divulge it to anyone else, not even my Uncle Luigi.' Joe said this in a slightly begging manner.

Claire, to tease him somewhat, suggested that they have a Welsh cake baking competition the following morning and if Joe availed himself, she would give him a copy of the recipe and the method. She emphasised that he was not going to have them until after the competition.

'Can I be the judge, please?' asked Ingrid. 'I know I am too young to be in the kitchen cooking, but I would love to assert the power of a judge.'

This was deemed be an excellent idea and furthermore, they would ask Cynthia and Ingrid's mother if they would like to take part. All was set for an American, Welsh, Norwegian bake off.

Bonnie, who had been stretched out on the carpet, awoke and sat in front of Joe. She then put her paw on his leg and, reaching up, tugged gently on his sleeve. Joe looked at Myfannwy, 'Does she want to go out, Myfannwy?'

'I wouldn't have thought so. She has only just been out for a walk.'

Joe, having had Bonnie tug on his sleeve a second time, rose from the settee. Bonnie then walked to the closed conservatory door and looked back at Joe. She sat and gave a bark.

'She obviously wants you to follow her into the conservatory.' Claire suggested.

Joe walked towards the conservatory door and opened it. Bonnie pushed her way inside and immediately jumped up onto the piano stool, one paw on the closed keyboard lid. Claire, Myfannwy and Ingrid had followed them into the room and were standing next to Joe.

'Oh Mum!' Claire exclaimed. 'Did you see that? She wants Joe to play.'

'Just like she did with Peter.' her mother added.

Joe was inquisitive. 'Peter?' he asked.

Claire replied. 'Peter was Bob's younger brother. He was killed in a road accident three years ago. He was a talented musician and would often play that piano. He was a lovely young man.'

'Claire is right, Joe. Like Bob, we regarded Peter as one of the family. He had a great sense of humour. We had some great evenings here at the Cwtch. The reason we were taken back is that Bonnie often did exactly to Peter what she just did to you.'

'That's incredible!' replied Joe. What do I do now?'

'She wants you to play.' Claire answered.

Joe sat down on the piano stool next to Bonnie. 'I think I am going to disappoint her.' he said as he lifted the cover.

Myfannwy suggested that Joe just play a few notes to please Bonnie. Joe pressed down on a few of the white keys, but it was not impressive. Bonnie thought so too by her reaction which was to give out a small bark.

'There you are! I told you she would be disappointed with it.' Joe turned to face Claire.

'I am not surprised!' was her unsympathetic response.

Joe turned back to the piano and looked at Bonnie. 'Okay Bonnie. Let me try something else.' Joe then proceeded to play a piece from Claire de Lune by Debussy.

What only his parents were aware of at that time, was that Joe was a talented pianist. He had been playing the piano since he was six. Claire and Myfannwy looked at each other in disbelief and Ingrid clapped. After a short, but impressive performance, Joe stopped playing and looked at Bonnie again. 'Was that better?' Bonnie barked.

During the time that Joe was playing, the rest of his family and that of Ingrid had returned to the Cwtch from their expedition and had taken up positions by the door. A round of applause came from all those present. Joe stood up and took a modest bow. Claire walked over to him and said, 'You kept that a secret, didn't you? Can you sing as well as you can play the piano?'

It was Joe's mother that provided the answer to her question. 'He is an incredibly talented pianist, Claire, but please do not ask him to sing. Whatever you do, do not ask him to sing.'

Joe was quick to respond. 'I am not a singer and before anyone asks me again, I am not going to be an elf! Let us go and get a drink!'

CHAPTER TWENTY-TWO
THE WELSH CAKE CHALLENGE

It was Wednesday, it was elf competition day, and it was the Welsh cake baking competition. Everyone was up early, and with breakfast over with, Claire stood ready to receive the competitors at the kitchen entrance. Myfannwy arrived first, followed quickly by Sofie and Cynthia. Joe arrived a couple of minutes later arm in arm with Ingrid.

'I hope you are not trying to coerce the judge, Joe.' Stated Claire.

'Ban him!' exclaimed his mother.

'I suggest we tie his hands together.' was the idea from Sofie.

'You lot think you're funny. You just wait and see who wins.'

Ingrid commented that his words were fighting talk. For the next couple of minutes Claire outlined the rules and said that she had prepared the ingredients for them individually and handed out pieces of paper to them with general cooking instructions. Joe had promised Claire that he would be putting pistachio nuts in his Welsh cakes just for her. This had left her yet again puzzled over the subject of pistachios but she said nothing.

It was when Sofie declared that she was going to put cabbage in her Welsh cakes that a huge gasp went up from the others. 'I am only joking! I am only joking!' she declared.

Except for Ingrid, they entered the kitchen and began to

bake. Ingrid went off to see if Henry would help her print some of her photographs. Two hours later the baking had been completed, the cakes had been put on separate plates, and cards, with their individual names on, placed under each.

Ingrid was summoned, whereupon she went about her judging duties diligently, but only after commenting that it looked like Joe had been in a snowman competition given the amount of flour he had spilt on himself. She was giving nothing away as she sampled each of the cakes on offer.

Finally, she declared the best Welsh cake by pointing to one plate. 'They were all very tasty I must say, but those were the tastiest.' Myfannwy took the card from under that plate and declared that Claire was the winner.

The next task they faced was tucking into the cakes with cups of tea whilst Ingrid clicked away on her camera.

After a few minutes had elapsed Joe walked over to Claire. 'Well done and look, all mine have been eaten as well.' He paused momentarily. 'You know, I think we should have a rematch but not here in your kitchen, in mine, in Snow Valley.'

Claire responded by saying that she would like that very much, but she would still win.

CHAPTER TWENTY-THREE
THE SLEIGH GOES MISSING

Just after lunch on that same Wednesday, Joe, Claire and Sandra were having a conversation in reception about the up-coming elf competition that evening, when Henry burst through the front doors, went passed them in a rush, and headed towards the lounge.

He was engaged in a conversation on his mobile with Sammy the Skip. They followed him into the lounge sensing that all was not well. Myfannwy, having heard the commotion, soon joined them.

Henry was sat on the settee with phone in hand and staring into the fire. His conversation with Sammy the Skip had ended.

'It's a disaster!' he proclaimed.

'What is Henry?' asked Myfannwy. As Henry was about to answer, Bob and Gregor walked into the room. They looked sheepish.

'The sleigh. It's gone!' Henry put the phone down on the settee and rubbed his brow. 'Stupid Sammy has swiped our Father Christmas sleigh.' Myfannwy had by this time sat down beside him. 'I shouldn't really blame Sammy I suppose. It's these two.' He pointed to Bob and Gregor. 'These bright herbs left the sleigh out in the yard for the paint to dry.'

'It makes sense to dry the paint outside, Dad.' Claire pointed out.

'Yes, I know, but they left it leaning up against the skip.'

'We are sorry, Henry. We were not thinking.' Bob looked at Gregor as he was saying this, and Gregor nodded his head in agreement.

'And Sammy thought that it had been put there to be collected.' Said Myfannwy.

'And that he did for sure!'

'Have you tried ringing him?' asked Myfannwy.

'Yes. I have just come off the phone from him. It took a long time for him to get back to me and by that time he had emptied the skip. What remains of the skip is now crushed and under a mountain of rubbish.' Henry looked at Bob and Gregor and shook his head. 'What do we do now?'

Bob had a suggestion. 'We could always build another one.'

Henry looked up at him in disbelief. 'It is now Wednesday, and the concert is this Friday. There's not enough time! Look how long it took you to make the one that just been destroyed.'

Joe intervened. 'Excuse me for butting in, but Bob has got a point, Henry. We could at least try.'

'Hear, hear, Joe!' exclaimed Myfannwy. 'Fighting talk! We can do it Henry. Let us have a crack at it.'

Henry stopped rubbing his brow, paused for a few moments and gave the project the thumbs up. Joe outlined what he thought should be the plan. He, Bob and Gregor would start first thing in the morning. They could not begin today due to the elf competition, but they had all Thursday and part of Friday to produce a brand-new sleigh.

Henry thanked Joe for his enthusiasm and support, to which Joe replied that he, Bob and Gregor, supported by plenty of coffee and snacks from the kitchen, would be the dream team. Claire confirmed that the supply of food and drink was not going to be a problem.

Henry offered his help, but Joe insisted that the dream team of three was all that was needed to come up trumps. Bob and Gregor expressed their agreement with that.

When all seemed as though it was heading in the right direction, Sandra hurried into the lounge. 'Henry. We have a problem! Maggie has just rung to say that Patsy has had an accident. She apparently cut her finger badly on one of the Christmas tree ornaments. She had to have stitches put in at the hospital. She's home now and resting.'

Myfannwy immediately headed out of the room. 'I am going to pop down and see her.'

'I'm sure she'll be fine.' Joe commented.

Claire, whilst concerned over her friend's accident, added that it left them with a problem for the Friday night. 'Claire will not be able to play the piano,' She turned to face Joe, 'but we do have someone who could deputise. Yes Joe?'

Bob spoke. 'What? Just like in the Westerns?' Henry shook his head again at Bob's remark. 'You ought to get a badge for it.'

Joe was also shaking his head. 'I can't do it. I don't know the arrangements.'

Claire suggested that he could go through those with Patsy

on Friday morning. She said please again. Joe paused for a second or two, looked at the faces staring at him in hope, and agreed he would try, to which Bob uttered, 'Just like the Westerns! Roped, thrown and branded, pardner. Yee Ha!'

Sandra was about to leave the lounge but remembered something else that Maggie had said. 'She warned us to look out for the Christmas tree tonight. She was still convinced that the tree was out to get her, but on this occasion, Patsy got in the way.'

CHAPTER TWENTY-FOUR
THE ARRIVAL OF THE ELVES

After the events of the day Wednesday evening was undoubtedly going to be a long and tiring one for those that were taking part. It was, however, regarded as one of the most enjoyable events in the village calendar.

The hall was due to open at six p.m. that evening but due to the buildup of numbers Patsy organised for it to be opened earlier at five thirty. As the party from the Cwtch arrived at the hall there was a line of adults and children waiting outside.

Many were there of course in elf costumes, but many others were dressed in alternative Christmas outfits. Claire herself had put on a Christmas outfit complete with Christmas hat.

Movement into the hall was speedy and soon the Cwtch party consisting of Sofie and Asgard Larsen, Myfannwy and John and Cynthia Bidder found themselves in the noisy, but joyful, atmosphere of the hall itself.

Earlier that evening Joe, Claire, Bob, Gregor and Ingrid had been given early access to assist in the preparations. Somewhere in the throng were Aggie and Maggie having one of their Aggie-Maggie conversations.

The organising committee and its band of helpers had transformed the hall into a winter and Christmas wonderland. The tree took pride of place on the left side and at the foot of the steps leading up to the stage.

It was covered in decorations and lights. Other decorations

hung from one end of the hall to the other. The stage as well was adorned except for the right-hand side which had been left empty awaiting the arrival of Father Christmas's sleigh from the inn.

Refreshments, including hot soup, were available on the tables lining the one side of the hall. On each table a small foot high Christmas tree had been placed, and all tables had been carefully decorated and lit with strings of fairy lights. Henry caught up with Myfannwy and between them they estimated that at least one hundred people were in the hall.

They spotted Joe and Claire standing by the piano with Patsy and made their way through the crowd to get to them. This took a little longer than it would normally because Myfannwy kept stopping to say hello to many of the assembled number on the way.

Patsy, complete with bandaged hand, greeted them. 'Hello Myfannwy. I see your guests have turned up in force.'

'You know what Patsy, they were all extremely excited about coming, and they seem to be getting on with the villagers very well indeed.' In the middle of the hall the Larsens and the Bidders were chatting to several of the vilagers. 'Where's Ingrid, Claire?'

Claire was about to say that Ingrid was about somewhere when Ingrid, camera in hand, appeared from out of the crowd. Henry commented that she had been taking lots of photographs already. Patsy asked Ingrid if she had enough memory cards for the evening to which the reply was. 'They are as bountiful as the number of cabbages in the Cwtch. I have seen how many there are in the storeroom.'

Myfannwy looked at Henry. Henry recognised the look. 'I

asked Ingrid to check that they were suitable cabbages for her family that's all. I am pleased to say they were but.'

'But what Henry?'

'I made the mistake of asking Bob to put the order through. He got confused and thought a dozen was fifty.'

'So, they delivered fifty cabbages, Henry?'

'It is okay really.' Ingrid interjected. 'My father has a great recipe for cabbage soup.'

The looks on the faces said it all. Henry wanted to avoid any further fall out, so he went off to find Bob and Gregor. Patsy said that it was about time she made her way to the stage to call the proceedings to order. She commented as she left that it looked like the elves had turned up in force and the natives now seemed restless.

Myfannwy took the opportunity to compliment her daughter on how she looked in her Christmas attire. Claire replied that she was going to wear a different one on Friday. Joe agreed that she looked wonderful, but it was still a pity that the hat was still too big for her.

'Still too big?' asked Claire.

'You know Claire. When I said the hat was cute, too big for you, but still cute.'

Claire replied that she could not recall him saying that. Joe simply responded with an okay. The conversation did not go any further because Patsy had now reached her position on the stage and was trying to gain the attention of the audience. Fortunately, Bob was on hand. He came across the stage, handed her a microphone, gave a short bow, and exited stage right. The crowd hushed.

'Thank you, Bob.' The microphone gave its obligatory one squeak and Patsy continued. 'Welcome everyone to our annual elf competition and Merry Christmas. I can see that we have quite a few elf costumes down there. You will be pleased to know that I will not be making one single elf joke this evening.' There was a chorus of hoorahs from the audience. 'As you may have observed I have hurt my hand and I shall not be playing the piano at Friday's concert.'

One single hoorah came from the audience. It came from ninety-two year and slightly hard of hearing, Kingsley Jessop. He apologised to Patsy when his ninety-three-year-old, wife, Gwendoline, clipped him around his ear.

'That's okay Kingsley. You are forgiven. The good news is that we have a young man who has stepped into the breach. Would you please put your hands together to thank Joe?' The audience clapped their appreciation and Joe acknowledged.

Now before we get down to the competition itself I have just a few brief announcements.' At this point, Kingsley shouted out hoorah and received a further clip around the ear from his wife.

'At the back of the hall and on the church notice boards are details of all the services being held in the church over the Christmas and new year period. Secondly, as you know. We have the concert on Friday, and I am still looking for anyone who can provide us with some entertainment. Please let me know by the end of the evening. I already have two parties that have volunteered their services.

Thank you Asgard for offering up your cabbage juggling act and thank you Maggie for what should be an interesting rendition of Silent Night.'

From somewhere in the back of the hall Maggie shouted. 'I forgot to mention vicar that there will be two of us singing. We've been practicing in secret, isn't it?'

'Excellent Maggie, responded Patsy, 'but are you sure about that. You haven't practiced the arrangement with me on the piano.'

'No need for that vicar. We'll be singing archie pelago, isn't it?'

Her pronunciation of A Capella gave rise to some chuckles from the audience.

'So, who is your singing partner, Patsy?'

'Can't say vicar. It is a secret for now. He wants to be a mini mouse.' Again, the audience chuckled at her pronunciation of anonymous.

Patsy turned her attention to the evening's events. 'I would like to express my thanks to all of you that have contributed to this year's events and thank you for your kind contributions of presents for the children. I nearly forgot to mention that the children will also be helping to entertain us on Friday with a selection of Christmas songs.

This year we have some special visitors with us. We have the Bidder family from America and.'

Maggie at this point turned to Aggie who was standing next to her. 'That's over the big pond apparently but it's not Farmer Myles' pond, isn't it?' Joe and Claire were heading out for some fresh air and were passing Maggie at this juncture. 'Isn't that right, Joe?'

'Absolutely correct, Maggie!' replied Joe. Joe and Claire stopped to be introduced to Aggie.

Meanwhile Patsy was continuing to talk about the international visitors. 'You may have noticed a young lady amongst you taking photographs. That is the delightful Ingrid, and she is here with her parents Ingrid and Sofie from Norway.' Maggie turned to Joe.

'Where is that Norway then, Joe?' she asked him.

'Oh. That is over another pond, Maggie.' Joe smiled.

'Yet another pond? I'd better get a map.'

Patsy could see everyone was itching to start the competition. 'Without further ado let us commence the competition. Would all elf competitors line up on the right-hand side of the hall facing the stage, please! Claire and I will start the judging and we will hopefully have a third mystery guest arriving soon to help us.'

She looked over to Henry for his confirmation. He put his thumb up to confirm this would be the case.' One final matter! We do not want a repeat of the goings on from last year. Remember it is Christmas. I call upon you all to.' Patsy paused to consider what to say but Maggie beat her to it.

From the back of the hall she shouted, 'Behave you little buggers.' and another hoorah went up from Kingsley. On this occasion he did not receive a further clip from Gwendoline. She had fallen asleep in her chair. Kingsley chuckled to himself at his good fortune.

Whilst the elves scrambled for position in the line, Claire who had returned to the front of the hall, joined Patsy at the table that had been placed at the front of the elf line. Maggie, having made her way to the table, posed a question to Patsy.

'Vicar. I know you are busy, but can I ask you an important question?'

'Certainly, Maggie.' Came the reply.

Maggie pointed to the tree on the other side of the hall and in a raised voice, which most of the persons present, could hear. 'Is that tree safe now? Look what it has done to you and we all remember that last year's tree murdered someone!'

'Maggie. How many times must I tell you? There was no murder!' At this point Maggie turned away from Patsy to address those around her.

'They hushed it up of course. I was going to get my friends in the regional police department to do something about it. I was going to, but then I realised that I did not know anyone in the regional police department.'

'Maggie. Again, there was no murder. The tree fell on Mr. Cole, true enough, but he was not seriously injured. In fact, he is over there munching on Welsh cakes.'

'Oh yes. That is right, isn't it? Sorry vicar.' Maggie turned away but, as she did so she shouted across to Mr. Cole. 'Oy, Ken! Remember! Do not go anywhere near that tree. Don't forget it killed you last year.'

Mr. Cole nodded, held up a Welsh cake, Patsy shook her head in disbelief, and another hoorah went up from Kingsley. He was enjoying his freedom.

CHAPTER TWENTY-FIVE
THE RISE OF THE ELVES

The hopefuls had lined up, Claire and Patsy had taken up their positions at the judges' table, and Ingrid was on hand to take photographs of the elves. Patsy beckoned the first candidate forward. The first elf approached the table.

He was dressed in a typical, but somewhat plain, elf outfit but as he approached the table, he placed a four-sided black bucket on his head. On each of the four sides was painted a face and each side had holes that coincided with the eye positions. Patsy looked at Claire. 'Here we go!'

'And you are?' asked Claire.

'I am the elf of a thousand faces. I am the Lon Chaney of the elf world. I can be Alf,' he turned the bucket around to next face. 'or Fred.' He turned the bucket again. 'or Larry or.'

Patsy intervened. 'Yes, we get the picture, but you only really have four faces, don't you?'

'Ah! But these are only four of my faces. I have the other two hundred and forty-nine buckets in my car. Shall I fetch them?'

Patsy responded immediately. 'No, that won't be necessary. Thank you. Thank you, elf of a thousand faces. We'll let you know!' The thousand face elf took the bucket off his head and walked away. 'It's going to be a long evening!', commented Patsy.

The next elf to approach the table was Dougie, Aggie's husband. He had obviously behaved enough to be allowed to attend. He was dressed as his favourite character Daft Invader. He had a black bucket, with holes for the eyes, on his head and he was covered in black bags from head to foot.

On the black bag covering his chest were the words, 'COUNCIL PROPERTY' and on his hands he was wearing ladies' black silk gloves. Next to the words council property there was a scorch mark. To add to his character, he started to breath heavily inside the bucket and brandished a painted mop handle as his weapon. Unfortunately, he had left the mop head on.

Despite the disguise Patsy recognised who it was. 'Hello Dougie. I see Aggie has let you come as Daft Invader Elf again.' Dougie realised that he had the mop head facing up, so he turned it upside down.

In a suitable voice he addressed Patsy. 'The farce is strong with you, vicar.' He was unaware of what he had said was wrong, Patsy smiled but said nothing about the farce.

'That will be him upstairs I guess Dougie. I see you have been fighting with your fighting sabre.' She pointed at the scorch mark on the black bag. 'Did you let your guard down?'

'Oh no vicar.' said Dougie, now in his own voice.

'Did someone strike you with their sabre?' Claire asked.

'No. That's where I caught it with the iron this morning when I was pressing it.'

Claire then pointed to the words on his chest. 'And what about where it says Council Property, Dougie?'

He replied that the costume came from the Jedi High Council

and not the local council as many would assume. He then added 'The farce does not seem so strong with you Miss Griffiths.' Claire replied that it was probably due to all the extra work she had been doing. They thanked Dougie and he left.

Ingrid had taken photos of each of the first two elves. 'This is even more fun than I expected,' she exclaimed, 'and I will take photographs of all the elves for my scrap book.'

CHAPTER TWENTY-SIX
HENRY'S MYSTERIOUS FATHER CHRISTMAS

Across the hall from the judging, Henry. Myfannwy, Asgard, Sofie, John and Cynthia had found a group of chairs together and were busily chatting. Cynthia had made the comment that she was particularly looking forward to the forthcoming Friday, the choir and the arrival of Father Christmas.

This comment prompted Myfannwy to nudge Henry.

'You haven't told our friends your other Christmas story, Henry.'

'That sounds intriguing, Henry. What is it? Is it another magical one?' asked Sofie.

'I bet it involves cabbages.' joked Asgard.

'No cabbages in this story, Asgard, but plenty of magical mystery.'

Myfannwy urged him to start the story.

'Okay.' Said Henry. 'And by the way I have witnesses to these events. It concerns the visit of Father Christmas to our Christmas Eve concert. Every year we hold the event and at the event every child in the village gets a present off Father Christmas. Well, Father Christmas has arrived promptly every year at eight o'clock.'

John commented that it sounded well organised.

'But that is just the thing, John. We do not know who this Father Christmas is. As you know' he winked. 'we have to arrange for someone to play Father Xmas because the real Father Christmas is too busy, elsewhere. Ten years ago, we arranged for Frank the Post to do just that, but he was not needed.

Before Frank could come onto the stage a figure, in all the Father Christmas regalia, just appeared from nowhere on the stage.'

John further commented that Henry was pulling their legs but Myfannwy confirmed that what Henry was saying was one hundred percent true. Henry continued with his story. 'Honestly, John. I am deadly serious. He was a perfect Father Christmas. He had the laugh, the looks and the kids just loved him.

After he had handed out all the presents, he danced off the stage and disappeared as quickly as he had appeared.'

Asgard commented. 'It was obviously someone who really want to be Father Christmas on the night.'

'That's right Asgard, and we dismissed it as a one off that first year. We never found out who it was. On that first occasion we did not get the chance to catch him, let alone talk to him.'

Joe who had by now joined them asked, 'What happened the following year?'

Henry continued. 'Again, we had arranged Frank to be Father Christmas and, to stop anyone getting on the stage. we locked and bolted all the doors leading to the stage. But there it was, a thump on the roof, and within seconds there he was again.

Frank was gutted I can tell you. He had practiced his Ho! Ho! Ho! hundreds of times.' Henry paused to get breath. 'We let him give out the presents so as not to upset the children and then he disappeared as he had done the previous year.

In fact, for the last ten years he just appears at the right time, gives out the presents, and leaves.'

'Has anyone attempted to stop him?' asked Cynthia.

'We tried, Cynthia, but you know what, none of us, except for Frank, ever thought it was the right thing to do. It was a magical experience every time and it just seemed right. The children loved him and, for the time he was here, there was always a really lovely warm feeling in the hall.'

Cynthia added. 'This village sure has its fair share of magic and mystery.'

'You are right Cynthia.' Henry commented 'Doesn't it just?'

CHAPTER TWENTY-SEVEN
THE ELVES MARCH ON

Back across the room Patsy and Claire had continued to see more elves but the judge that Henry had arranged had still not made an appearance. The next elf approached the judges' table. He was dressed up in what appeared to be a super-hero elf outfit.

'So, you want to be one of our elves on Friday to help Father Christmas?' asked Patsy.

'I am Super Elf, here to help Father Christmas and save the world in general.'

'To save the world as well! That is mighty ambitious, Super Elf.' commented Claire.

'I go wherever I am needed, helping the needy and thwarting evil, provided there's a reliable bus route to get me there and back.'

Patsy was intrigued to know what his super-powers consisted of. 'What would just one of your super-powers be? Pick your best one.'

Super Elf thought for a moment. 'My wife says that I am particularly good at doing the dishes.' Patsy thanked him and he left.

A few yards away John Bidder had been talking to some of the villagers that were standing around. He spotted, close by, a man dressed in green hat, green shirt, green jacket and green trousers. 'Hey there my friend! Shouldn't you be in the line over there?

John pointed to the line of elves queuing up.

The man asked why. 'Well, I think you might get selected in that elf costume. It's darn good!'

With a look of disgust on his face the man faced John. 'I would have you know that these are my everyday clothes.' Having been insulted by John the man walked away.

'Whoops!' exclaimed John.

Patsy and Claire, helped by cups of tea from Myfannwy, continued their work to find the half dozen or so elves for the Friday. Their next elf candidate approached. He was dressed in an elf onesie.

'Good evening, ladies. I am Cedric so people call me Cedric.'

'I see Cedric,' said Claire, 'that you have come in a onesie outfit. Well, welcome to you. Now Cedric, or shall I call you Onesie Elf, what qualities do you think you have to be a Father Christmas helper?'

'Oh. I did not think this would be an interview. Should I have prepared? Should I have brought a C.V.?'

'No, that's fine Cedric. Your outfit is certainly novel.'

'It should be. I knitted it myself. Unfortunately, I have not completed the left foot yet. I ran out of wool, but please be assured that I will have finished it by Friday.'

Patsy was studying his outfit in detail.

'Will it not be a little hot for you on Friday. You are perspiring quite a bit now Cedric, and when you finish your outfit, it will be even hotter inside there.'

'I have a plan to counteract that! I am going to sew pockets inside the onesie and fill them with ice cubes.'

'But they'll melt surely?' asked Patsy.

'They would, wouldn't they? I will go away and do some more planning. Thank you for the interview.' Onesie Elf. as he was now known. walked over to get some refreshments to cool him down.

CHAPTER TWENTY-EIGHT
HER LADYSHIP

Matters in the village hall were clearly hotting up, particularly for Onesie Elf, but back at the Cwtch, things were a lot calmer and tranquil. Kenneth was in the bar area and Sandra was on duty in reception. Bonnie was asleep in the office. Whilst Sandra was catching up on some paperwork a news item appeared on the television that was positioned at the end of the desk.

It was a broadcast from one of the region's broadcasting channels. A well know news reporter presented the item.

'Newport police are tonight still seeking the driver of a Volvo bearing Norwegian number plates that shed its load of cabbages on the exit of the Newport services earlier in the week. Police patrol officer, Mustafa Green, said that in his twenty years on the force he had never before experienced an incident involving cabbages on his patch.'

Sandra was oblivious to what was being said on the television, but she was aware that a car was pulling up in the car park just outside the main doors. Following on from an earlier telephone call the Cwtch was now expecting the arrival of a Lady Angela Mirley, and Sandra suspected that the car held that very person. What she did not know was that the occupant in the car was Elizabeth, Claire's identical twin sister. Neither would she find out that it was Elizabeth for some time.

The reason for that was Elizabeth, who had continued that Sunday train journey on to Swansea to meet friends, had conjured up a plan with her fiancé to arrive at the Cwtch in disguise.

Gerald her fiancé, who was also Elizabeth's theatrical director, had easily persuaded her to disguise herself as the Lady Angela Mirley, the fictitious character that Elizabeth would be playing on stage in London from January.

Gerald was given the use of his father's Rolls Royce which added to the deception. He was to be the chauffeur.

Her friends in Swansea, fellow thespians, ensured that through the theatrical makeup, clothing, and helped by the hat that covered at least a third of her face, anyone would find it difficult to recognise her. The real question was whether her friends and her family at the Cwtch would see through her disguise.

She had however been practicing her 'posh' voice as she called it, and it certainly disguised her real Welsh voice, the voice that Joe had heard in the train.

As the car drew up, Gerald, who had driven the car from Swansea, turned to Elizabeth who was sitting in the back. 'Are you ready, Liz?' he asked.

'I am more than ready. Let us do this!'

Gerald, now acting the part of Cozens the chauffeur, and Elizabeth, now playing the part of Lady Angela Mirley, stepped out of the car. Sandra would be their first test. They walked through the entrance doors and Elizabeth, followed by Gerald. walked up the hall to the reception desk. Sandra looked up, smiled, and said good evening.

'Good evening my dear. I am Lady Angela Mirley. You were expecting me?'

Sandra replied that indeed they were. 'Everything has been

arranged for your stay. Did you have a pleasant journey?'

'My dear. In a Rolls Royce you always have a pleasant journey.' So far so good. The disguise was holding up. Elizabeth looked around.

'I expected it to be busier than this. Are people staying away for some reason?'

'No. It's not that your ladyship.' Sandra replied. 'Most are down in the village hall at present. We are holding the annual elf competition this evening.'

'How quaint!' Elizabeth paused for a moment. 'Do you have your own chef here at the hotel?'

'We do. Claire, Mr. and Mrs. Griffiths' daughter, is our resident chef but she is down at the village as well.'

'Anyway, my secretary phoned earlier in the week to make my reservation. I have been given a room of a high quality, one assumes. I do not want just a standard room.'

'I think you will find the room to your satisfaction but if there is anything you need, we will do our best to accommodate you.'

'One hopes so. Incidentally, I forgot to mention that I would be accompanied by my chauffeur, Cozens. With her left hand, and in almost dismissive manner, she pointed to Gerald. 'Can you find a room somewhere for him. Anywhere will do.' Sandra glanced at Gerald and he raised his shoulders.

'I'm sure that it will not be a problem, your ladyship,'

'And please my dear, ensure that he is billed separately. He gets paid an allowance to cover that sort of thing.'

'I understand. Would you be requiring a meal tonight, your ladyship? Molly is in the kitchen so she can prepare one for you.'

'Have one delivered to my room at nine o'clock precisely. Do you have a menu?'

'You will find one next to the phone in your room.'

'Cozens can make his own arrangements with you later.' insisted Elizabeth.

'If you would just sign this card your ladyship, I will arrange for someone to take your luggage to your room.' Sandra passed the card and a pen to Elizabeth who signed it with her left hand whilst pointing at Gerald again.

'No need.' She said, 'Cozens can do that. Well, go on Cozens. Get the luggage from the car.' Gerald was pleased with the acting performance of Elizabeth. There was no doubt about that, and thus far, their charade had fooled Sandra. Gerald left to retrieve their luggage from the car. 'Is the bar open? You do have a bar, I hope?'

Sandra took the signed card from Elizabeth and passed her the room key. 'Yes, we have, and it is open. Kenneth, our bartender is on hand. Kenneth was going to be Elizabeth's second test. Although Elizabeth had known Sandra for a long time she still was well known to Kenneth.

Elizabeth was enjoying herself as Lady Mirley. 'Is it possible that I could be brought a drink, my dear?' Sandra suggested that she escort her to the conservatory where she could relax and have a drink brought to her by Kenneth.

'That sounds reasonable. I will have a large gin and tonic and please ensure that there is no ice, and that it is in a tall glass. Sandra noted that this was the first time that she had said please. She escorted Elizabeth to the conservatory where Elizabeth sat in one of the armchairs out of the direct glare of the lights.

'I will get Kenneth to bring you your drink immediately.' Sandra headed off to Kenneth to arrange the drink.' Once she had left the room Elizabeth looked around, adjusted her hat, and smiled broadly. It was still a case of so far so good.

CHAPTER TWENTY-NINE
EDDIE THE ELF

Meanwhile, back at the village hall, there was still no sign of Henry's mysterious third judge and Patsy with Claire had talked to at least twelve elf hopefuls so far. The next candidate strode towards the judges with a beaming smile on his face. On his jacket he had emblazoned the words 'A REAL ELF DOES NOT FEEL THE COLD.'

'Hello. I am Eddie the Elf. How are you both this fine evening?'

'We are fine, thank you Eddie.' responded Patsy. 'Is that true? That real elves do not feel the cold?'

'It certainly is! It is one of the ways to tell the difference between an elf and let us say a non-elf.'

'That is a really great elf costume.' remarked Claire.

Eddie, now with an even broader smile replied. 'Thank you so much. I had a special lady tailor it for me.'

Claire continued with the questions. 'And where do you live Eddie?'

'I move around quite a lot on assignments, but currently I am on holiday here in Pontynant.'

'Where are you staying?'

'Oh! you know. Here, there and everywhere. We elves have a saying that wherever you lay your hat that's..'

Patsy was keen to finish his sentence. 'Your home?'

'Not exactly. Wherever you lay your hat that is where you are sleeping that night. I'm taking a little break from my normal Christmas job.' Eddie knew he was allowed one or two fibs a year and he had just used his first.

'I see,' replied Claire. 'and you are available Friday to help Father Christmas?'

'I promise you that on Friday I will be one of the best elves you will ever have had. I think I know how Father Christmas likes things done, and I know how to manage the children. I will not let you down. I will not let Father Christmas nor the children'

He paused for a moment and then continued. 'I've actually been here before, you know. Well nearby. It was a fleeting visit quite a few years ago. I was on a mission to help someone out.'

'Well thank you, Eddie.' Patsy looked at Claire and smiled. Eddie thanked them for their time and started to walk away but Ingrid stopped him.

'May I take your photograph, Mr. Eddie Elf?' she asked.

'You may Ingrid, but please would you take one of me standing between these two lovely judges?' Claire and Patsy stood either side of Eddie and Ingrid took the photo. Claire then took a photograph of Eddie standing next to Ingrid.

With the same beaming smile that he had earlier, Eddie turned, said goodbye, and walked away across the hall.

Patsy, on noticing that Ingrid looked a little puzzled, asked, 'Is everything okay, Ingrid?'

Ingrid replied. 'How did he know my name?'

'Oh! Someone must have told him earlier.' suggested Claire. Claire then turned to Patsy. 'I think he has got to be a definite choice. There's something about him!' Both Patsy and Ingrid agreed. 'I reckon we grab a cup of tea and march on. I see Bob is next.'

Ingrid offered to get them the tea so they continued with Bob. When she returned with the drinks Claire and Patsy sipped them and talked to Bob at the same time.

Eddie who had made his way across the hall stopped next to Henry and said, 'Hello Henry.'

'Do you think you will be chosen?' Henry asked him.' You certainly look the part and what does that say on your jacket?' Eddie told him that it read 'A real elf does not feel the cold'.

Eddie went on say. 'I am glad to see your fractured ankle mended okay.'

'Fractured ankle? I had that accident years ago. How did you know about it? Henry looked perplexed.

'Yes. It was some time back, wasn't it?' remarked Eddie.

Suddenly Henry realised where he had read the words before. They were the words that were written on the jacket of one of the elves that evening when he was a boy, the night the Christmas tree was planted outside his bedroom window.

'You were there!' Henry gasped.

'Sure, was Henry. Nice to see you again.' At this Eddie walked away leaving Henry speechless but somehow content.

CHAPTER THIRTY

DECEPTION WITH A GIN AND TONIC

Contentment was the name of the game as far as Elizabeth was concerned. Gerald had joined her in the conservatory, but their conversation ceased on the entrance of Kenneth. He was carrying a tray on which there was a gin and tonic in a tall glass.

'Your drink your ladyship. No ice and in a tall glass as requested.'

'Put it on that table. That is kind of you. It's Kenneth is it not?' asked Elizabeth.

Kenneth put the drink on the table next to her. 'Indeed, it is! Can I get you anything else, my lady?'

'I may want another G & T in a little while. Do you have a little bell that I could summon you with?'

'I don't, I'm afraid, but I shall check in on you shortly though.'

'Very well. You do have sufficient stock of gin and tonic for the coming week?'

'Rest assured our cellar has been fully stocked.'

Elizabeth was becoming even more confident in her new role. She believed she had now fooled Kenneth. However, it was put in doubt when Kenneth asked her if he had met her before. Quick thinking Elizabeth went on the attack.

'Perhaps you were serving at the bar at Ascot or perhaps Badminton, or Henley even?' She looked closely at Kenneth for his reaction.

'I don't get to attend those types of functions, your ladyship.'

'Then it's highly unlikely we have crossed paths before, one feels.' Her responses seemed to have deflected Kenneth's suspicions and after he was out of earshot, Elizabeth gave an enormous sigh of relief.

'You are doing very well, Liz.' Gerald whispered. 'You are a great Lady Angela Mirley. That's exactly how I want you to play it on stage.' Elizabeth smiled and sipped her drink. Gerald went off to the bar to get a drink for himself.

CHAPTER THIRTY-ONE
THE INTRUDERS

The remaining elves were queuing up to see Claire and Patsy when the doors at the back of the hall were flung open with an almighty crash and a trio of youths, clearly intoxicated, entered. Each was holding a bottle of beer. As they moved further into the hall people moved out of their way.

On this happening, Patsy made her way hurriedly to where they stood. One of the youths was standing slightly in front of the other two.

Patsy was now standing directly in front of the first youth. 'I'm sorry but you will have to leave.' She spoke this in a very stern manner. She meant business.

'The leading youth stared at her, wobbled a little, took a swig from the bottle and spoke. 'Who says so?'

'I do.' Patsy responded. 'No alcohol is allowed in this hall and you are all clearly drunk.'

'What's going on here then?' he shook his bottle at the surroundings.

As he was saying this Joe and John had made their way to where Patsy was standing but she stopped them going any further. Patsy pointed to the first youth.

'You are obviously out to cause trouble. I am asking you again to leave.'

'You and your friends don't frighten us. Eh boys?' The two other youths echoed their agreement.

'Then I shall be calling the police.'

'P.C. Plod? We do not care. Give them a call. Let us all have a good laugh.'

Maggie who had also made her way to just behind Patsy addressed the first youth. 'You're from Llanelli, aren't you?'

'Llanelli? What are you on about, oldie?'

Joe told him to be respectful and get out.

Joe received the response. 'Oh, shut up! Anyway, we are from Pontypridd as it happens, not Llanelli. We are the Pontypridd three. We were the Pontypridd four, but Neville is inside now.'

One of the other youths took a small step forward. 'Yeah. Inside his house. His mother wouldn't let him out.'

The first youth pointed to the elves. 'At least we don't dress up in silly costumes. What are they supposed to be over there?'

Ingrid who had now come to stand by Patsy could not contain herself. 'They are elves. Nincompoop!' The first youth turned his attention to her.

'Another foreigner! Elves? They look more like. Um. more like.' He was in mid thought trying to find the right expression when the second youth interrupted him.

'Garden gnomes, Cyril?'

Patsy was getting to the end of her tether but continued

to stop anyone else getting involved. 'Look Cyril. It's time you were gone!'

The first youth, now known to everyone as Cyril, seemed not to pay any attention to her. 'I think you're all stupid.' He shouted. 'And just look at that hat.' He first pointed at the hat that Ingrid was wearing and then knocked it off her head. 'On the floor that's where that should be.'

With that comment he trod on it, but again, despite the likes of John and Joe wanting to get involved Patsy ushered them to stay back.

Bob, still in elf costume, was getting a bit hot under the collar at the youths' antics and strode forward only to be greeted by the first youth pointing at him and saying, 'And who do we have here then?' He turned to the other two youths. 'Hey boys it must be Arnie the Elf.' This caused the other two youths to snigger.

At the other end of the hall, Sofie, when she realised that Ingrid had been treated badly, decided to act. She tugged on Henry's sleeve and told him to make his way to the main light switch and when he got there, he was to wait for her to nod to him. When she did, he was to turn the lights off, count to two, and turn them back on again.

Henry, although puzzled at what she had asked him to do, agreed to do what she wanted. The first youth continued to hassle Patsy. 'There you are then. You're all scared and you're all silly village people.'

He had only just finished his sentence when there was a loud bang from the other end of the hall. Sofie had picked up one of the miniature Christmas trees and had banged it down on the table next to her.

This immediately grabbed the attention of everyone in the room. She began to walk towards the youths. As she passed the second table, she banged the tree down on that and at the same time picked up a string of battery-operated fairy lights.

She passed the third table and then the fourth table, banging the tree down on each. An eerie silence had by this time descended on the hall.

Claire, who had walked over to where Asgard was standing, asked him if they should stop Sofie. He turned to her, and with a big smile on his face said, 'Best not!'

Sofie was now standing immediately between Patsy and the first youth. Having checked that Ingrid was okay, she began staring at the youth. She spoke firmly but quietly to him. 'At this moment in time I am your worst nightmare.' The youth just looked at her and laughed.

Asgard turned to Claire. 'He should not have laughed, I am thinking!'

Sofie stood her ground with no sign of humour on her face. 'We are here to have a peaceful Christmas and you are being a 'rompe'. In your language that is an a*s*, and I'm going to do something about it.' Again, the youth laughed in her face and again Asgard repeated to Claire that he should not have done that.

Sofie then turned her head towards Henry and nodded. He did as he had been instructed. After a count of two the lights came back on. Within those few moments a groan was heard coming from the direction of the first youth. The youth was still standing in front of Sofie, but he was now in some pain. His hands had been tied together with the string of fairy lights and

Sofie had implanted the Christmas tree, reverse way up, down the back of his trousers.

The second that the lights came back on there was also an immediate gasp from those in the hall when they saw what Sofie had bestowed upon the youth. To add to his embarrassment Sofie reached up to where the switch was on the lights and turned them on. 'Happy days, rompe, and be grateful that there wasn't a star on the top of the tree.' She then turned to the other two youths. 'Do your friends want an early Christmas tree present as well?' They backed away and Asgard smiled at Claire.

Maggie tapped Aggie on her arm. 'Well bless my soul! Now we know how to deal with people from Llanelli. I would have stuck a pen up his nostrils if I had had a pen that is.' No sooner had she finished speaking when several pens appeared out of nowhere and landed at her feet.

Patsy did, however, persuade her not to do anything. Myfannwy, who had now been joined by Asgard and Claire turned to Asgard and exclaimed, 'I must eat more cabbages!' Asgard nodded his head.

CHAPTER THIRTY-TWO
ARMY RE-INFORCEMENTS

The first youth was still standing, but in a great deal of discomfort and his two colleagues were nearby cowering, when the army major and his men entered the hall.

'You could not have timed your entrance any better, Major. We are having some difficulties with these three.' Patsy pointed to the three youths. 'Sofie here is our saviour with what she did with the tree.'

'Yes, I can see that Patsy.' The major took a good look at the reason for the youth's distress. 'The old Christmas tree down the trousers manoeuvre, eh?' He looked at Sofie and asked, 'Norwegian army?'

Sofie stood more upright. 'Yes major, Captain Sofie Larsen, Brigade Nord, retired.'

'You sly old thing you!' Patsy commented.

'Thought so! Seen that one before when I was in your country. Now Patsy I will get my men to sort these three out for you.' The major turned to the sergeant. 'Sergeant, you and the men take these reprobates outside and deal with them.' Patsy pointed at the major and insisted that there should be no violence. 'Minimal force, sergeant.'

'Yes sir!' replied the sergeant. 'Minimal force, it is.' He saluted the major, barked his orders to his men, and the youths were escorted out of the hall, one youth more slowly than the other two.

The major watched his men carry out his orders and then turned to face Patsy. 'My men and I were wondering whether your offer of hot soup was still available.' Patsy replied that it was, but just as she was saying this a scream of pain emanated from outside the hall. She looked at the major and said, 'Major?'

He suggested that it was only his men retrieving the Christmas tree. This was substantiated when the corporal, carrying said item, marched back into the hall with the somewhat disheveled tree in his grasp.

'One Christmas tree duly extracted, sir.' He stood to attention in front of the major and saluted. The major returned the salute and suggested to Patsy that perhaps she did not want the tree back. She shook her head, and the major gave the order to the corporal to dispose of the tree.

Another exchange of salutes took place, and the corporal left the hall. The major further suggested that he and his men drop the youths off at the nearest police statio n.Patsy was about to say that she agreed with that when another scream of pain came from outside. The corporal re-entered the hall.

'Tree now returned to where we found it, sir.'

'Jolly good! We will take your offer of soup up some other time, Patsy. By the way, our regimental dinner is being held in Cardiff in January. Would you like to accompany me?' Patsy smiled and said she would be delighted. 'I'd better be off then.'

The major then turned to face the rest of the people in the hall, saluted, wished everyone a merry Christmas as well as wishing Ingrid and her mother God bagatelle. Sofie was about to tell him that it meant merry trifle when Ingrid tugged her sleeve, turned to the major, and wished him God bagatelle.

CHAPTER THIRTY-THREE
A CHANGE OF JUDGE

The minute that the army major had left Patsy sought out Henry to enquire as to where the third judge was. She emphasised that Claire and she had been up to their eyes and needed help. He had that moment just taken a call from that person and he had rung to say that his car had broken down and would not be able to get there. Henry apologised.

'That is okay, Henry.' Patsy said. 'I have just had an idea!' Before Henry had time to ask her what the idea was, she had walked away and was heading towards the stage. At the top of the steps, she picked up, and turned on, the microphone. She tapped it to get the attention of those in the hall. Silence fell in the hall within moments.

'Excuse me ladies and gentlemen. Unfortunately, our third judge is not going to make it tonight, so I am going to enlist the aid of Sofie in the judging. Are you okay with that Sofie?' Sofie nodded that she would be willing.

'I would like to say two more things. Firstly, Sofie will have the final, final say on who is selected. Secondly, I would like to point out that there are plenty of those table Christmas trees left, if you know what I mean. Would all those in favour of Sofie being our third judge and having the final say please raise your hands.' The response was immediate. Every single person in the hall, within a split second, had raised their hands. 'That's unanimous then. I had the feeling that it would be.'

Claire, Patsy and Sofie made their way back to the judges' table and Patsy beckoned the next elf forward. The next elf entry was in fact a man in a suit carrying a ventriloquist dummy.

'This looks interesting, ladies.' Patsy observed. 'Hello, good evening, and you are?'

The man pulled up a nearby chair, sat down, and positioned the dummy on his lap. The dummy was dressed in full elf costume and it was the dummy that answered. 'Are you speaking to me or him?' Sofie confirmed either could answer. 'In that case,' said the dummy, 'I'm the brains behind this outfit so it's me then. My name is Dalton. His name is.' He paused. 'What is your name again?' Dalton turns his head towards the man.

'I am Terrence as well you know.'

'Right, I do the talking, yes?' Terrence nodded.

Claire took this as the hint to talk to Dalton. 'How long have you been an elf, Dalton?'

Dalton replied. 'About two hours, and before you say it, I know I look stupid!'

Patsy, whilst smiling at Terrence, reassured Dalton that he did not look stupid at all and in fact looked quite cute. Dalton first looked at Terrence and then looked at Patsy. 'I like you. This is just one of my many costumes. I have been dressed as a clown, a chef, a gentleman's gentleman, a horse, a monkey and in fact you name it I have been it, and now an elf. What is the world coming to?'

Terrence folded Dalton and put him in his bag. As he did so Dalton said, 'Here we go again. Into the bag. I never get to find out how much we get for any of these gigs.' Terrence had put him in the bag with his head sticking out of the top.

Claire put it to Terrence that he was in fact a professional ventriloquist. Terrence, in his own voice answered. 'Yes, I am. I have been doing it for several years now. Dalton in there is my favourite character but please do not tell him. I am Terry Brookman. It is a pleasure to meet you.' Speaking to Sofie directly he said that he had been totally impressed by the way she had handled the youths earlier.

From inside the bag, Dalton shouted, 'Creep. Didn't see you go to help her!'

Patsy highlighted to Terrence that no payment was being made to the elves.

Terrence replied, 'I know. I am down visiting my parents for Christmas in Llandodwin, just down the road. I saw your poster in a shop window last week and thought I would come along.'

Claire added to what Patsy had just said. 'The problem we have Terry is that we need the elves to help Father Christmas hand out the presents. It might be a bit difficult for you with Dalton?'

Patsy turned to Claire and Sofie and whispered a suggestion. She turned back to Terry. 'I have an idea. Would you consider giving up some of your time on Friday to entertain the kids?'

'I would love to!' was the reply.

Patsy thanked Terry for coming, apologised to him again that he could not be an elf, or rather Dalton could not be an elf, but they would see him on Friday. Terry got up from his chair, picked up the bag holding Dalton and turned to go. From the bag Dalton spoke. 'How much did we get Terrence?'

Terrence in his own voice replied that it was a freebie, to which Dalton replied, 'Not another one! You are too much of a soft touch, not like me. I'm hard.' Terry looked back at the three judges.

'He will have settled down by Friday.' Terry reassured them.

Sofie commented that she still had a spare Christmas tree for Dalton if he misbehaved. The judges, looking at Dalton's head sticking out of the bag saw him cross his eyes and heard him gulp. Dalton and Terry were going to be one of those entertaining on Friday along with Asgard and his cabbages, the children choir, and Maggie and her anonymous friend.

The judges had by now seen thirty-two elf hopefuls and had just one left to talk to. Patsy beckoned her forward. She was in the thirties and she was dressed as a very glamorous elf. Dalton, earlier, had already commented on her figure.

'Girl Power!' exclaimed Claire. 'You must be a model when you are not an elf!'

'I'm not actually.' came the reply. 'I was not sure if you were accepting female elves. By the way, my name is Gillian.'

'We certainly are Gillian.' said Claire. 'If you are not a model, what do you do, Glamorous Gillian?'

'I am a funeral director in Barry.'

Patsy spat out the coffee she was drinking. 'A what?' she asked.

'A funeral director.' repeated Gillian. 'I don't dress like this of course when I'm doing my work.'

'I would hope not!' exclaimed Patsy. 'I wonder what would happen if you did. The mind boggles. I think if you tone down your costume a tad, I do not see why you cannot be one of the elves. The toning down might also prevent Father Christmas having a heart attack.'

Claire and Sofie agreed with this but Claire had one final question. 'I must ask you Gillian how did you become a funeral director in the first place?'

Gillian replied, 'I inherited the business undertaking from my father.'

That was it! The three judges went into the customary huddle and decided on the five elves for the Friday. They were to include Glamorous Gillian, Eddie, Bob, and two other villagers. They had ruled out Daft Invader because they thought he would frighten the kids with his costume and ruled out Super Elf just in case his superpowers were called upon elsewhere.

Sofie climbed the steps to the stage and with the aid of the microphone announced the winners. There was obviously a mixed reaction to the results, but no one seemed to want to argue with what Sofie had announced. Jokingly she had carried one of the small Christmas trees with her up onto the stage. This might have had something to do with it.

The elf competition was at an end and people were making their way out of the hall. Claire, Joe and Ingrid were the first from the Cwtch to leave. Henry, Myfannwy and their other guests had agreed to stay on a while longer to help Patsy clear up.

CHAPTER THIRTY-FOUR
HER LADYSHIP IS IN FINE FORM

Joe and Claire, with Ingrid holding their hands, made their way back to the Cwtch. They discussed the evening's events and Ingrid confirmed that she had taken many photographs. At reception Sandra asked how it had all gone and Claire gave her a two-minute review of the events.

'Wow!' exclaimed Sandra. 'I will want to know more. By the way Claire, Lady Penelope and Parker have arrived. They are in the conservatory.'

'Who are Lady Penelope and Parker when they are at home?' asked Joe.

'She means Lady Mirley, and Sandra, I am assuming that she has brought a chauffeur with her?'

'Yes, that's right Claire. Poor person. Who would want to be her chauffeur?'

'Well, I am going to get some food on the go in the kitchen. Come on Ingrid. You must be starving. I'll see her ladyship later.' The two disappeared off in the direction of the kitchen.

'And I,' said Joe 'want to meet this Lady Penelope.'

'Don't forget Joe. It is Lady Angela Mirley. The Lady Penelope thing was a joke.'

'I know. Puppet, right?' He headed off towards the conservatory.

Inside the conservatory Elizabeth and Gerald were discussing quietly how well things were going. They reverted to character when Joe entered. Elizabeth was still in full costume and makeup and Gerald had suggested that she put on her shaded glasses and tilt the hat a little more to enhance the disguise. He was still in his chauffeur's uniform.

As Joe entered, he said hello to them both. Elizabeth immediately recognised Joe from the train, but it was a complete surprise that he was here at the Cwtch. Joe, on the other hand did not recognise Elizabeth as his Welsh pistachio lady.

'May I join you?' Joe asked.

Elizabeth without thinking said. 'You're the American!' She was about to finish the sentence by saying 'from the train' but realised in time. Fortunately, Joe just took it as her knowing that there were Americans staying at the Cwtch.

'Yes, I'm from the States. I am over here with my parents on vacation. I was just admiring your set of wheels outside.'

'One doesn't drive one-self, you understand. One leaves that to Cozens over there.' She said this whilst pointing to Gerald and with her left hand picking up her gin and tonic.

'Are you staying at the Cwtch for long, your ladyship?'

'For a week or so.'

'I know you have just arrived but what are your first impressions of the Cwtch?'

'One must say that I am used to bigger establishments of a higher quality, but it had to be a last-minute booking so one has to go with the flow.'

'I must say I love it here. Henry, he's the owner is a great guy, and his wife is a peach.'

'A peach?' Elizabeth had never known her mother referred to as a peach before.

'She sure is. The people here bend over backwards to help, and they are very friendly.'

'But what about the quality of the food?'

'They have a wonderful young lady in charge. She is the daughter of Henry and Myfannwy, the owners. Her food is tasty and is always of a high standard.'

'One shall see if you are correct in due course, young man. From which part of America are you from?'

'I'm from Pennsylvania, your ladyship.'

'I have never been there. Has it been civilised yet?'

'Why of course! Have you been to the States at all, your ladyship?'

'Yes of course. Mainly New York. My first husband was an American. He took me there on his business trips. I did not like the place at all.'

Rather sarcastically Joe responded. 'Why? Too many Americans? Could I ask what your husband did for a living?'

'He was into property, stocks and shares. Very boring to me but he was phenomenally successful at it and the money just kept coming in. Now that part of it I did like.'

'So, you didn't get to see the West Coast?'

'Oh no! One gets the impression it is brimming over with actors and the like. I abhor actors. So pretentious!' It was at this point that a muffled cough came from Gerald. He was finding it hard not to join in the fun that Elizabeth was clearly having.

Elizabeth turned to Gerald. 'If you have a dry throat, Cozens, why don't you go and get yourself a drink. You can get a drink for me at the same time and one for Mr., Mr?'

'Call me Joe please. Mr. Bidder is too formal. I will have a scotch please. Thank you.'

Gerald was about to leave when Elizabeth stopped him. 'And make sure they charge your drink to your account. Charge Mr. Bidder's drink to my account. And no ice!'

Gerald grabbed his opportunity to participate more in the charade. 'I will indeed ensure the division of cost, your ladyship.' He bowed to Elizabeth, and knowing Joe was looking elsewhere, smiled and winked at her. She smiled back. A few minutes later Gerald returned with the drinks and handed them out.

Elizabeth continued in the guise of Lady Mirley. 'My first husband, I should say my late first husband, was a ghastly man. Rich, but he had terrible manners and, would you believe it, took ice in his drinks.'

At this point, Ingrid, carrying her camera, came in with Bonnie. Bonnie naturally recognised Elizabeth and immediately ran up to her. The disguise did not deceive her! Elizabeth wanted to make a big fuss of Bonnie but had to restrain herself, to stay in character. She did however pat Bonnie on the head.' Ingrid pulled Bonnie gently away from Elizabeth and told her to sit and stay a few feet away.

'The establishment allows dogs then?' Elizabeth asked. 'Unfortunately, this dress cost me well over a thousand pounds.' Elizabeth thanked Ingrid and asked her where she was from.

'My name is Ingrid. I am from Norway.' Joe pointed out that Ingrid should address her as your ladyship, so Ingrid repeated what she had just said and added your ladyship to the end. 'I am here with my parents. May I take your photo for my album, your ladyship?'

'I am sorry, my dear. I hate having my photograph taken. I hope you understand.'

'That's alright.' Ingrid replied.

Gerald asked Ingrid if she wanted a drink.

'I would like a glass of lemonade, please.'

Gerald headed off to get Ingrid her drink. Joe took the conversation back to Lady Mirley's husband. 'You mentioned that your first husband was American. Am I to assume that there is a second husband?'

'Was Mr. Bidder. Was! He was Lord Mirley, and he was English.'

'Was?'

'Yes, he has been deceased now for some time. He died in what one could only describe as a climbing accident. He was a very keen climber you know.'

'May I ask where the accident happened? The Alps, the Andes, Everest?'

'Heavens no! It was in Kensington.'

'Kensington? Kensington in London?' Elizabeth could see that she had Joe on the hook again.

'Yes.' she replied.

'I didn't think there were any mountains in Kensington, a couple of hills perhaps.'

'It was not on a mountain, young man. One evening, he was coming back from his Chelsea club totally inebriated, not, it must be said, an infrequent situation, and decided to climb up the outside of our apartment building. The silly fool was trying to carry two bottles of bourbon at the same time.

To cut a long story short, Mr. Bidder he slipped and fell to the pavement. He was.' Elizabeth looked at Ingrid and decided to change what she was going to say. 'He had perished before one could say Jim Beam.'

Gerald returned with Ingrid's drink and was accompanied by Claire. Elizabeth huddled closer into her armchair and pulled the hat further over her face. This was going to be the real test. This was her identical twin sister after all.

'Welcome to the Cwtch Inn, Lady Mirley. I am Claire. My parents are down in the village at present, so they apologise for not welcoming you personally. As soon as they return, they will come through to welcome you properly, I am sure.'

This was it. Elizabeth was going to try out her Lady Mirley

voice out on her sister. 'I suppose that will have to do then. I may have retired by that time in which case I shall expect to see them in the morning.' Elizabeth was becoming a little nervous and thought that she should keep the conversation to a minimum. She raised her left arm almost dismissively.

Claire thanked her and apologised that she needed to go back to the kitchen. With that, Claire turned and headed off in that direction. The gasp of relief from Elizabeth was almost audible. She seemingly had passed muster. She had hoodwinked her sister it seemed.

'That was the cook then?' she asked.

Joe pointed out that she was more than just a cook. 'She's a chef, your ladyship. A talented chef at that. She also has an extremely attractive personality to boot.'

'You said that with a bit of a sparkle in your eyes, Mr. Bidder. Do I sense you have some feelings towards my,' Elizabeth again stopped mid-sentence. She was about to say sister but thought quickly and said, 'my host's chef'. 'Anyway, does the hotel have any Michelin stars?'

'I don't think so.' Joe replied.

'Then I shall judge the quality of her food in due course. Now, I am going to retire to my room for the night. One is rather tired. Cozens, you can escort me to my room and here, carry my coat and scarf please. Also, confirm with the girl on the desk that I shall be phoning down for a meal and a drink shortly. You can sort yourself out!'

Before Elizabeth left the conservatory, Joe had one final question for her. 'Before you retire, may I ask you a rather personal question, your ladyship? You obviously did not get on with either of your husbands. Why marry them in the first place?'

Elizabeth wanted her last line of this act to be good one. 'My dear boy! For the money of course, for the money!' She and Gerald then left the room, exit right as Gerald would normally have said.

Joe, Ingrid and Bonnie were left in the conservatory. Bonnie had wanted to follow Elizabeth, but Ingrid had restrained her. Except for Bonnie, Elizabeth had fooled everyone. How long would it last?

CHAPTER THIRTY-FIVE
THE DAY'S END (NEARLY)

It was nine-thirty when Henry and Myfannwy, together with the Larsens and the Bidders left the hall. Myfannwy felt that there would be time for everyone to have a meal and a drink back at the Cwtch. Bob, Gregor and Maggie were staying on longer to help Patsy. Henry informed Myfannwy that he had received a phone call on his mobile from Sandra saying that Lady Mirley had arrived, accompanied by her chauffeur.

When they arrived back at the Cwtch Sandra updated them on Lady Mirley having retired to her room, and that Claire was now with Ingrid and Joe in the conservatory. To give Claire a break Henry and Myfannwy decided that they were going to prepare a hot buffet for those that wanted one, but before they disappeared into the kitchen, they ensured that Kenneth was ready with his pen and pad to take a drinks order. Ingrid, Claire and Joe had by now moved into the lounge and were soon joined by John, Cynthia, Asgard and Sofie. All looked tired but all were in good spirits.

'We understand you have been entertaining a lady of the realm.' Sofie said to Ingrid as she gave her a hug. Joe commented that he was not sure whether it should be called entertaining. She was a strange lady full of airs and graces.

Ingrid added, 'I would say she was an en merkelig gammel, a strange old duck.' Sofie scolded her gently over this comment but Joe came to Ingrid's defence by saying that she had summed up Lady Mirley perfectly. Joe looked at Ingrid and smiled.

Sandra had been told by Henry that she was to finish her shift and join everyone for a drink. She and Kenneth entered carrying trays with the pre-ordered drinks on them. These were gratefully received. Sandra sat next to Claire and asked about the elf competition.

'Was there any fighting?' she asked. Claire replied that there had been none and suggested that Sofie was the reason for that. Sofie laughed and said that she enjoyed herself.

'I could not get over how many different elves there were.' remarked Sofie. 'What was that one that Bob said drove off in the big Bentley? 'she asked. Claire looked at her. Sofie continued. 'It was the one late on that you and Patsy said reminded you of someone from your British royal family. Prince.' Sofie was halted by Claire's interjection.

'No! It could not have been him, surely? Would he have said that he had better get back to the other half before he was missed?'

'The other thing Bob said was that he had a driver and what looked like, what do you call them, bouncers, with him. Oh, and the car had a flag on the bonnet.' Claire gulped and tried to persuade herself that it could not have been who she thought. Claire was awoken from her thoughts by Sandra. 'I bet there were some funny moments down there in the hall.' Claire and Ingrid gave her the highlights.

Sofie asked Claire who the person was that was dressed as a rugby elf and who had gone away crying with his mother when he realised the concert was on Friday and he could not make it. Claire said she did not know. She had not recognised him as being from the village. The answer to who it had been came from Henry as he and Myfannwy entered with trays of hot buffet food. 'That person in the rugby elf costume plays as a forward for the senior Welsh rugby union squad, would you believe?'

Henry, Myfannwy and Claire were the last remaining people in the lounge and were discussing their plans for the next few days when Sandra appeared at the door.

'Just as I was leaving Henry, the phone in reception rang. It was Lady Mirley's chauffeur. He has asked if you, Myfannwy and the cook would go to her room immediately.'

'Cook! What is that all about? 'asked Claire in a slightly upset manner.

'That sounds like we have been summoned.' said Myfannwy. 'I suppose we should see what she wants.' Declared Henry. 'Let's go!'

CHAPTER THIRTY-SIX
LADY MIRLEY REVEALED (BUT NOT TO ALL)

The three headed off to Lady Mirley's room not knowing what to expect. Before knocking, Henry expressed his hope that everything was okay, and Claire suggested she was about to complain about the food. Myfannwy was a little calmer than the other two and simply said. 'Let us see.' She then knocked on the door and the chauffeur let them in.

The room was only partially lit, and Elizabeth was sat in an armchair away from the door. She had removed all her facial makeup, but the clothes, hat and glasses remained. Again, the lighting and the hat draped over the face made it difficult for anyone to see her face. Her parents and sister were standing just inside the room.

Gerald, who was still in his chauffeur's uniform was the first to speak.

'May I present to you Lady Angela Mirley.'

Henry responded with, 'Good evening your ladyship. I apologise for not greeting you personally earlier. I hope you have found everything to your satisfaction.' Elizabeth said nothing. Gerald however spoke on her behalf. 'Her ladyship has found everything quite adequate.'

'Just quite adequate?' asked Myfannwy, quite disappointed at the description.

Again, Elizabeth remained silent, and it was Gerald that spoke. 'You must understand that her ladyship is accustomed to staying in five-star hotels which have Michelin star restaurants.'

At this point Elizabeth coughed and this was her cue to Gerald to take proceedings to the next stage. Gerald turned to face Elizabeth. 'I do apologise to your ladyship for failing to introduce you with your full title.' He paused and turned to face Henry, Myfannwy and Claire again. 'May I introduce to you Lady Angela Gwendoline Mirley,' he paused. 'of Pontynant.'

Henry looked confused, Myfannwy was bewildered, and Claire was lost for words.

Elizabeth rose out of the chair and took off her hat and glasses and spoke in her normal voice. 'I am the Lady Mirley of Pontynant. Hi mum, hi Dad, hi Sis.'

There were hugs and tears for the next few minutes and when things had settled down Elizabeth explained all, including the fact that Cozens the chauffeur was in fact Gerald, her fiancé of a few days and Lady Mirley was in fact the character she would be playing in London in January.

There were more hugs and this time they included Gerald. This re-union went on for an hour longer, but ended with Henry saying that they would have a good catch up the following day.

Just before Claire left Elizabeth thought it best to tell Claire about the train incident with Joe and the fact that she had met him as herself and not as Lady Mirley. Claire was intrigued but agreed that they would have a good chat over breakfast.

Another thing they agreed on was that Claire was not to tell Joe who Lady Mirley really was. There was further mileage to be had from the deception.

CHAPTER THIRTY-SEVEN
IT'S A NEW DAY AND A NEW SLEIGH

Early the following morning Claire had risen to prepare an early breakfast for Joe. He was meeting up with Bob and Gregor a short while later to start work on the new sleigh in the workshop. She, in her full chef's clothing, sat next to him as he was devouring his full cooked breakfast.

On seeing her parents coming into the reception Claire got up from sitting next to Joe and ushered her parents back into the hall.

'There's nothing wrong, Mum.' she whispered. 'But you're not to say to Joe that Lady Mirley is actually Lizzy.'

'Why ever not, Claire?' asked her mother.

'Lizzy and I are going to have some fun with it.'

'You two girls! Neither of you has changed. 'Don't go too far. You know he is fond of you.'

Henry thought about it for a moment and, with Myfannwy, agreed to go along with it. Claire thanked them and went towards the kitchen to get them some breakfast. Henry and Myfannwy joined Joe in the dining room.

'We feel a little guilty getting you to do all this work for us.' Said Myfannwy. 'This is after all supposed to be your holiday, Joe.'

'No worries. I promised Mum and Dad that I would spend

more time with them next week so they are happy, and don't worry Henry, the boys and I will get the sleigh completed.' Henry thanked him. 'Hey, I had better get going.' He grabbed a few mouthfuls of coffee and headed out of the dining room.

He exited the dining room and walked briskly down the hall to the reception. He was in a hurry and focusing on the task ahead of him. Elizabeth, who had been told by Sandra incorrectly on the phone, that Joe had left the building, had decided to come down to talk to Sandra and explain the plot that she and Claire were to hatch.

She was now not in disguise and was wearing tee-shirt and jeans. As they were talking Joe appeared. Sandra exclaimed that she thought he had left already. He replied that he was now going and without a moment's thought gave Elizabeth a peck on the cheek. 'See you later and thanks for breakfast.' He then ran down the corridor and out of the main doors. He was running late.

After he had left reception Sandra turned to Elizabeth,

'Clearly he still isn't aware of who you are.'

'Judging by that kiss, that's right.' replied Elizabeth as she walked off to the dining room. 'So far, so good!'

Outside the inn, Joe stopped to adjust his coat, but looked back at the doors because something was bothering him. He was puzzling over how Claire had changed so quickly from her full chef's uniform into the tee-shirt and jeans that he saw her in when she was in reception? He did not, however, have time to dwell on it. Gregor and Bob came marching up to him.

'You look deep in thought there, Joe.' Bob observed.

Joe responded. 'Yes, Bob I am. I just cannot understand how she changed so quickly.'

'Women eh partner? Full of surprises! I remember my first girlfriend did not talk to me for a week.'

'How come she didn't speak to you for a week?' Joe asked.

'She had gone on holidays with her mother. Gone for a week she was!'

'Okay!' Joe looked at Bob and then at Gregor, who was as much in wonder as Joe was. 'Anyway, no time to waste. We have a sleigh to build.'

As they began to walk off in the direction of the workshop, Bob had a question for Joe. 'Bob, can I ask you a question?' 'Certainly' was Joe's reply. 'In America you drive on the right, yes? Well, if you are driving on the right how come you don't hit the cars coming towards you?'

'That's not how it works, Bob.' Joe replied. 'They are also driving on the right.'

'That's exactly my point! That has got to be dangerous!'

'I'll explain later. Let us get this sleigh made.' Joe wondered if Bob had any other such questions.

A few minutes after Joe and his work team had left for the workshop Henry and Myfannwy were eating their breakfasts in the dining room. Elizabeth and Claire were at the other end of the table and were chatting away. No other guests had yet come down for breakfast. Elizabeth was continuing to tell her sister about her encounter with Joe on the train.

'So, there was only one packet of the pistachio nuts available, and I was adamant that I was going to have them.' Elizabeth explained.

'Of course! That explains why he was talking about pistachios.' Claire remarked.

'And not only did he call me the Welsh pistachio lady, but he had a go at my Christmas hat. He said it was cute but too big for me.' Elizabeth caught the attention of her parents. 'Mum, Dad. Are we all agreed that for a while we do not let on to Joe that I was, am, Lady Mirley?' Claire commented that although it was a bit cruel, she was up for it, but Elizabeth needed to avoid him for a while longer while they plan what they are going to do to wind him up.

Myfannwy pointed out to them that Joe was bending over backwards to help and that it was a little unkind to torment him. However, she went on to say. 'Provided we do not prolong his agony too long, I will go along with it.'

Henry who had a huge smile on his face said. 'I will go along with the plan, and can you imagine his reaction when he finds out you two are identical twins. I must be there to see that. I think we need to forewarn the other guests, especially Joe's parents and we'll get them to promise that they will not let the cat out of the bag until the time is right.'

A few minutes later Gerald, now not in uniform, came into the dining room and they updated him on their plan. Soon after, the Larsen family, accompanied by the Bidders, joined them. Claire and Elizabeth jointly outlined what they were proposing to do with Joe, and Joe's parents both thought it was a fun idea. Sofie and Asgard stated that provided John and Cynthia were for it they too would not reveal anything.

Ingrid was a little more hesitant about the plan but with the reassurance from both Claire and Elizabeth that they would stop if at any point Joe was finding it too much, she agreed.

Whilst the plan was being formulated in the dining room, Joe, Bob and Gregor had donned their work clothes and were discussing how they were going to proceed. Joe took the lead, 'Right guys, we have today to complete the sleigh and I would like to get the sleigh to the village hall by tonight. I'm going to be tied up tomorrow morning with piano practice.'

'What do you want us to do first, Joe?' Bob asked.

'You and Gregor collect all the materials that you think we will need.'

Bob confirmed that there should be enough timber and boards in the back store.

'How about electrical items, do we have any?' Joe asked.

'I have plenty to do the job. I am electrician.' said Gregor proudly. 'Twenty years in Polish shipyard as head sparkifier.'

'Where in Poland did you come from Gregor?' asked Joe.

'Gdansk. I am Grzegorz Gerik Gorski from Gdansk'

'That's quite a mouth full!'

'That is why people call me Gregor or GG.'

Joe responded. 'Then I will call you GG. I am relying on you and Bob to pull this off today.'

'No problem, Joe. You can bet on this GG.'

'And I am going to be called Bob for the job.' Bob was not going to be left out when it came to titles.

'Okay. Right, before we start let me have the schematics that you had for the previous sleigh.' Gregor and Bob looked at each other. 'The drawings?' Bob walked to the workbench and brought back a small piece of paper on a clipboard. It was a picture cut out from a magazine of a sleigh. 'And that's all you have?'

Gregor replied. 'We just improvised as we went along.'

Sympathetically, Joe put forward his idea. 'Here's the plan then. You two collect all the materials and I will use that paper over there to sketch out a design. It is seven o'clock now, get the materials together by eight, yes?' Bob and Gregor agreed and disappeared into the store. Joe sat by the bench and started sketching.

Within twenty minutes Gregor and Bob has amassed a huge amount of timber, MDF boards and electric cabling in the centre of the workshop. Joe showed them the sketches that he was working on and work began in earnest. It was lunchtime before they knew it and the sleigh construction was going well.

At lunchtime, Claire and Molly entered, carrying trays on which there were meals and flasks of coffee for the three workers. 'Lunch is served.' Claire announced. 'Molly and I have made you some roast beef sandwiches and there are some Welsh cakes as well. Oh, and some handwipes for you to clean those hands.'

'Thanks both.' said Bob, as he and Gregor took the trays off them.

'How is it going, guys?' Claire asked.

Joe answered. 'I think we are getting there, but it will be a full day I'm thinking.'

Molly and Claire then left the workshop and the team to enjoy their break.

'These are superb sandwiches, Joe.' Gregor commented, with a mouthful of sandwich.

'We are being spoilt. I should have asked for Ingrid's favourite food.' Joe said.

'What is that then, Joe?' Bob asked. Joe informed him that it was rice pudding and cured cod. Joe was getting to know Bob well by now, and as Bob raised his head to ask another question, Joe second guessed it.

'And before you ask, Bob. The fish had not been ill.'

Bob nodded and kept on eating. When their lunch break was over, the three went back to work and carried on till five o'clock. Again, Claire and Molly brought them food and drink to sustain them and the three carried into late evening.

At eleven o'clock Joe declared that they had worked on the sleigh long enough. It was complete all bar the paint drying. Bob and Gregor, shattered as much as Joe was, went off to their respective homes. Joe walked wearily back to the Cwtch.

Joe was thankful that he had remembered the front door key because all occupants of the Cwtch had by now retired to bed. Once his head hit the pillow Joe was fast asleep. It had been a long hard day but at least the finished sleigh was safely locked up in the workshop.

CHAPTER THIRTY-EIGHT

A VISIT FROM THE POLICE

The following morning Joe's alarm clock went off at the preset time of eight o'clock. Although feeling the tiredness of the previous day's endeavours he managed to freshen, dress, and arrive in reception by eight thirty. Kenneth was standing in for Sandra on reception duty.

Joe stopped to talk to him. 'And how are you this morning, Kenneth?'

'I am fine. Thank you, Joe, and your good self?

'I am shattered! The boys and I did not finish the sleigh until gone eleven last night. The good news is that it is finished. We left the paint to dry overnight. Indoors this time and hopefully the guys have transported it to the hall this morning.'

'Well done. Everyone will be pleased.' Kenneth commented.

'Talking of everyone, where are they?'

'Either in the dining room or lounge.' Kenneth replied.

'And her ladyship?'

Kenneth, who had also been enlisted into the twins' deception plan, replied that she had not graced anyone with her presence yet. He knew that Elizabeth was staying in her room awaiting confirmation that Joe had left the building. Kenneth added. 'She requested breakfast be delivered to her room this morning.'

'I would have loved to have carried on the conversation that I was having with her on Wednesday evening but yesterday she wasn't around when I left for the day, and she had retired when I came in last night. That lady is full of surprises!'

Kenneth smiled knowingly. "Oh! You can say that again!'

'Right. Let's go say hello to the folks and give them an update.'

Joe entered the dining room to find Henry, Myfannwy, Claire and the Larsens sitting around the table enjoying breakfast. 'Morning everyone. Everyone is up nice and early!' He remarked as he sat next to Claire. He received a chorus of 'good mornings' back. 'No parents?'

'They are in the lounge. Joe.' Claire informed him. 'They had early breakfasts. Talking of breakfast, I will go and rustle something for you. Pancakes?' Joe nodded to approve the choice.

'How did you get on yesterday Joe?' asked Henry. 'Didn't see anything of you after breakfast yesterday.'

'As of now, Henry, the completed sleigh should be sat on the hall stage. It was a great team effort. By the way we uncovered and old Rudolph reindeer model in the stores so we fixed that up as well.'

'Excellent Joe! Henry's face lit up. "We owe you!'

Joe continued. 'Gregor was planning to complete the lights on the sleigh this morning and guess what? He has even managed to install a remote control for the lights. One switch turns the sleigh's main lights on and the other turns on the red light that he fixed on as Rudolph's nose.'

'That is fantastic! Exclaimed Myfannwy. 'We appreciate what you've done for us.'

'No worries, Myfannwy. Once I finish breakfast, I will disappear off to the hall to go through the piano arrangements with Patsy, but while Claire is cooking up the pancakes, I'll pop in to see how Mum and Dad are doing.' Joe updated his parents on what had happened the previous day and returned to the dining room to have his breakfast when Ingrid summoned him.

So far no-one had revealed what was going on behind Joe's back. There had certainly been smiles and chuckles between them when Joe was not in their company. There was no doubt about that. Joe devoured his pancakes, drank his coffee and bid everyone a farewell. On his way out of the dining room he turned. 'I'll be in the hall for the rest of the morning. I'll come back for lunch at one o'clock if that is okay, Claire.' Claire shouted after him. 'Not a problem!'

When Joe arrived in reception Sandra had replaced Kenneth on duty. 'Oh, hello Joe. Kenneth told me you finished the sleigh. Well done.' Before Joe could respond, the front doors were opened and in came the mother of Jeremy, accompanied by her police constable husband. P.C. Thorncroft. Mrs. Thorncroft was carrying a small brown paper bag.

As they approached the reception desk Sandra, who knew both well, spoke. 'Good morning Mrs. Thorncroft, Officer Thorncroft. Can I be of assistance?'

'Hello Sandra, we understand there is a young American staying here at the Cwtch?'

'That might be me. I am the only one that fits the bill. I'm Joe Bidder.'

'Are you the gentlemen that was talking to my son outside the butcher's shop the other day?'

'Jeremy?'

'Yes. Mr. Bidder, Jeremy has told us that when you were talking to him, he mentioned that he had told you he was being bullied in school.'

'That's right.'

'We were of course aware that this was happening, and we have asked the headmistress to investigate.'

'We have to go through the correct channels as you must appreciate.' Her husband added. 'Jeremy also told us that you advised him to hit the bully back the next time the bully hit him.'

'I am so dreadfully sorry. I realise I should not have said that. I over-stepped the mark.'

Mrs. Thorncroft continued. 'Yesterday in school, Jeremy hit the boy back. Gave him a bloody nose, he did.'

'We cannot condone Jeremy's action of course.' P.C. Thorncroft added.

'Is he in trouble? Am I in trouble?' Joe asked.

'Jeremy has been suitably reprimanded.' Mrs. Thorncroft replied.

'Now it's my turn I guess.' Joe suggested.

'As I have just said we do not condone Jeremy's course of action, but we would like to thank you.' Mrs. Thorncroft started to smile.

'Thank me? I did not expect that!' Joe was taken back by her comment.

'It turns out, however, that it did the trick. Jeremy and Jason are now sitting next to each other in class and would seem to be striking up a friendship.'

'Though, I would recommend that you do not give out such advice in future. On this occasion all has turned out okay.' This time P.C. Thorncroft had a smile on his face.

'So, I am off the hook as it were?' asked Joe, looking somewhat relieved.

'Yes.' P.C. Thorncroft confirmed.

P.C. Thorncroft nodded his head. As she was about to turn to leave Mrs. Thorncroft remembered that she was holding the bag. 'I nearly forgot, Mr. Bidder. Jeremy wants you to have these.' She handed Joe the bag and Joe took from it a small model of a turkey and a small model of an ostrich. 'He said he wanted you to have them so that you would know the difference between the two. I do not know what that is all about, I am sure, but he said you would understand?

'I certainly do! We had a debate on Monday whether the bird hanging up in the butcher's shop was a turkey or an ostrich. He claimed it was an ostrich.'

'Ah!" Exclaimed P.C. Thorncroft. 'Now, that may be my fault. As a wind up I told Jeremy that it must be an ostrich because it was so big.'

Mrs. Thorncroft looked at her husband. 'Richard!' With that they turned and left.

'Phew!' exclaimed Joe. 'I thought for a moment that I was going to be in police custody over Christmas.'

'Or worse! You could have been doing bird. It means being in prison!'

'I know. Very apt, Sandra, and very droll. I will see you at lunchtime.'

Joe exited the building and strolled down the drive to the village hall. Sandra watched him leave and ensured that he was well on his way. Once this was established, she rang Elizabeth to say the coast was clear, and then made her way to the lounge where everyone had gathered after breakfast.

Within the lounge, the Griffiths, the Bidders minus Joe, and the Larsen family were sat around the lounge, with Bonnie lying in front of the fire. They were waiting for Elizabeth and Gerald to join them before they discussed the strategy surrounding the hoodwinking of Joe. Various matters were being discussed, the food, the sleigh, Ingrid's photographs, Patsy's accident, the squirrel, Maggie, the Pontypridd three, Sofie's battle tactics and of course the elf competition.

The various conversations stopped when Elizabeth and Gerald joined them. They were both dressed in their casual clothes. Lady Mirley and Cozens had been parked in their wardrobes. After all the greetings had been completed Henry stood up in front of the fire.

'Good morning everyone. I hope you all are having a happy stay at the Cwtch. I know Myfanwy, Claire and I have thoroughly enjoyed having your company. Can I remind everyone that we have the concert this evening and I know we are all in front of a treat in that regard.' Henry looked towards Elizabeth and Gerald. 'As you all now know our other lovely daughter Elizabeth and her fiancé Gerald have joined us for Christmas.'

Cynthia apologised to Henry for interrupting. 'Myfannwy! I cannot get over how alike Elizabeth and Claire really are. It is incredible.' Myfannwy smiled and commented that, as young girls, they often used the similarity to fool people.

This prompted Henry to bring the subject around to Joe. 'As you are now all aware the twins have hatched up a plan to have some fun at Joe's expense. I will let Elizabeth and Claire say more about this in a minute, but first I want to say that we have all agreed not to take it too far, isn't that right girls?'

'Yes, Dad.' answered Claire. 'Joe is coming back here at lunchtime and after just one more little prank we will tell him.'

'That is right, Dad. We will not prolong his agony for too long.' added Elizabeth with a broad smile on her face.

At John's request, Elizabeth and Claire, between them, went over the events of the last few days that had led to this situation, and then explained what they had planned for Joe at lunchtime. Everyone was happy with their intentions and knew what the stage instructions were for each of them. Ingrid added that she thought Joe would take it in good heart.

Gerald stepped forward when the girls had finished. 'I know we must avoid Joe seeing us this morning, but Liz and I are going to take the Rolls for a spin after. Does anyone want to come?' Ingrid was the first to put her hand up, followed closely by Sofie and Cynthia.

While all this was going on Joe had arrived at the village hall and had started going through the arrangements with Patsy, who was still nursing her bandaged arm. Bob and Gregor had brought the sleigh safely to the hall and it now stood in its final position on the stage. They were now installing and testing the lights on the sleigh and Rudolph's nose.

Maggie, who had come to the hall with Patsy early that morning, expressed the desire to sit in the sleigh, so carefully avoiding the tree, she climbed the steps, walked across the stage and plonked herself in it. Bob and Gregor smiled when she gave it her seal of approval.

Several other villagers were in the hall cleaning, polishing and arranging the furniture in readiness for the evening. Kingsley, and his wife, accompanied by their sixty-five-year-old son Charles had brought in some freshly cut flowers from their garden. The flowers were being arranged in vases around the hall.

Patsy and Joe worked tirelessly for the rest of that morning and at half twelve they decided enough was enough. Everyone went their separate ways, and the hall was locked up by Patsy with the intention of it being re-opened early evening.

Back at the Cwtch the stage had been set and all the actors knew their roles and their positions.

CHAPTER THIRTY-NINE
JOE FINDS OUT THE TRUTH

Sandra patiently waited at the main doors on lookout duty and when she eventually spotted Joe at the end of the drive, she hurried back to the lounge to tell everyone. At this cue Elizabeth, who had dressed up in Claire's chef outfit, and Gerald, clad once more in his chauffeur's uniform, positioned themselves in front of the reception desk. Sandra had returned to her customary position behind the desk.

All the others were in the lounge except for Claire who had secreted herself away in the kitchen. The plan called for her to be in tee-shirt and jeans.

As Joe walked into reception, Gerald and Elizabeth were in a passionate embrace and were exchanging kisses. Joe's heart sank as he saw, who he thought was Claire, kissing this man, this stranger, who had only just come to the Cwtch.

He thought Claire and he had been getting on well, but this incident had shattered that belief.

He strode quickly passed, ignoring Sandra's 'welcome back', and headed towards the lounge. Seeing the assembled throng there he continued into the empty conservatory followed by Bonnie. Once inside, he shut the door and sat at the piano somewhat forlorn. He opened the keyboard lid and started to play random individual notes.

Back in the lounge there was a subdued silence, Cynthia was the first to speak. 'I think Elizabeth and Gerald have hit a nerve there. I'll go and get Claire.' Joe was still playing random notes when Claire entered the conservatory. He looked up as she came in and then reverted to looking at the piano keys.

'Are you okay, Joe?' she asked.

'I'm fine.' Was the somewhat abrupt reply.

'You are clearly upset.'

Joe looked up again, but this time with a puzzled expression on his face. 'How do you do that? How do you manage to change so quickly all the time?' Claire did not answer. 'What was that all about with that chauffeur? I thought we had something going.'

'I thought so, also.' Claire replied.

'Clearly we have not!' By this time, the others had entered the conservatory and were standing just inside the doors. Elizabeth, still in Claire's chef clothes, was standing behind them out of Joe's vision. 'You're not jealous Joe, are you?' asked Claire.

Joe continued but in a quieter tone. 'I'm astonished and disappointed that's what I am. That chauffeur, a complete and utter stranger has only been here a day and he is hitting on you.

What is worse is that you were kissing him. I thought that when I invited you back to Snow Valley you would realise my feelings towards you.' Gerald stepped forward and to the side of the piano. Joe pointed towards him. 'And you! What was that in reception, buddy? Hitting on Mr. and Mrs. Griffiths' daughter like that.'

Gerald replied. 'So? I kissed their daughter.'

Joe looked at him in disbelief. 'And what do you think Lady

Mirley will say when she finds out what you have been up to?' Elizabeth, still standing out of sight from Joe, took this as her prompt, and in her Lady Mirley voice, spoke from behind the others. 'One already knows.'

Joe looked back at Gerald. 'Now you're in for it pal!' As he was saying this Elizabeth made her way to the front of those by the door and Myfannwy walked towards Claire and put her arms around her. This was the height of Joe's confusion and bewilderment. One moment he was looking at Elizabeth and the next Claire. He was looking at the identical twins, but the penny was not dropping. He was speechless as well as dumbfounded.

Myfannwy spoke next. 'Joe, if he had kissed this daughter, I would have been upset but he didn't, so I'm not.' Myfannwy made it clear that she was referring to Claire by hugging her a little more. Ingrid said it was time to make everything clear to Joe.

Claire was in complete agreement. 'Joe, this is my twin sister Elizabeth. Lizzy. We have fooled you by getting her to dress up in my chef's uniform.'

Elizabeth walked over to the side of Gerald. 'Hello Joe. I am pleased to meet you for the third time, American.'

Joe admitted that he still found it confusing. 'Three times?' he enquired.

Claire explained that in addition to meeting Elizabeth properly today, he had met her for the second time the previous night. She went on to explain that Elizabeth had fooled them all in the guise of Lady Mirley and that Lady Mirley was her new role in the West End. Joe's jaw dropped even further but he was gradually seeing the light.

'You're the actress of course.' he paused. 'But when was the first time I met you? Oh, my Goodness, on the train of course!' The penny had reached its destination. 'You're the Welsh pistachio lady! I remember!' He paused and looked around at all the smiling faces around him. 'So, this has been one big wind up, eh?'

'Sorry Joe but we couldn't resist it.' Claire declared. 'And Gerald there is Elizabeth's fiancé.'

Gerald added his apologies for being part of the scam. 'And can I just point out that it was you, Joe, that kissed my fiancé yesterday morning in reception.' Joe remembered that he had kissed the person he thought was Claire as he was leaving to meet up with Bob and Gregor.

'Oh boy! Sorry about that.'

'Joe was slightly embarrassed. He then turned to face the twin that he was told was Claire. 'But really how do I know you are Claire?' Claire went up to him and kissed him. Joe declared that he still was not sure. This prompted to kiss him again much to the amusement of those in the room.

Joe looked at Bonnie. 'Is this Claire, Bonnie?'

Bonnie barked.

'There is another way you can tell them apart. Joe.' stated Myfannwy. 'Elizabeth is left-handed. Claire is right-handed.'

'Oh! I nearly forgot, Joe,' Elizabeth approached him and handed him, with her left hand, a packet of pistachio nuts. 'Now you are going to share those with me, aren't you?'

Joe smiled and answered immediately. 'Nope!'

Henry was relieved that everything had worked out and the

lovely, relaxed atmosphere had returned. 'To the bar everyone, but only for one. We have a long evening ahead of us.'

The afternoon, after everyone had been suitably fed, was one of relaxation for all.

CHAPTER FORTY
THE CONCERT BEGINS

At five o'clock Henry and Myfannwy left the Cwtch and headed towards the village. Accompanying them were the Larsen family and the Bidders, John and Cynthia. Claire, Joe, Bob and Gregor had left earlier to help Patsy and the other villagers make the final preparations for the hall's official opening time of five thirty. Elizabeth and Gregory said they would be down at opening time.

By five thirty there was a line of individuals eager to gain access. This queue included the children from the village and of course Maggie. At the front of the queue stood Kingsley and his wife Gwendoline and when Patsy opened the doors he shouted 'Hoorah!' Gwendoline did not, on this occasion, clip his ear. Kingsley stood out particularly as he had dressed as a Christmas elf. Indeed, a large proportion of those waiting to go in were dressed in Christmas attire.

By six o'clock the hall was well populated, the Children's choir was in position, and Joe was sat at the piano with the hand-bandaged Patsy going through their final preparations. Elizabeth and Gerald arrived and made a beeline for the piano, at which Claire was now standing. Patsy took up her position on the stage and announced the evening's entertainment was now going to start. Having checked with Joe, she announced that the choir would now sing Jingle Bells. The singing began and when they had finished. they received a huge round of applause.

The next person to entertain the hall's occupants was Asgard with his Norwegian King cabbage juggling act. His three-minute continuous juggling routine, without a spill, brought about a rapturous response.

When he had finished Patsy thanked him and ensured those present that he was using out of date cabbages. The cabbages that he had used would be donated to Maggie for her chickens.

Maggie shouted from the back of the hall. 'Thank you, vicar. I take my hat off to you. I would if I had a hat that is, isn't it?'

As the children began their rendition of 'Away in a Manger' Patsy, helped by Claire, picked up the cabbage bits that had fallen on the floor. Throughout the time that Ingrid had been in the hall that evening she had been continuously taking photographs.

Whilst the choir was singing, Henry checked with Bob and Gregor that all the lights functioned and that the switching on of the lights would work. He received a positive and confident response. Henry went away happy and joined Patsy at the foot of the stairs.

"Everything has started well, Henry.' Patsy commented. 'Oh! By the way. Bob and Gregor ensured me that all the presents had been put inside and behind the sleigh.' She added that all the elves had turned up and were ready for action.

'Excellent.' Henry replied. 'Thank you, Patsy. As they spoke Bob approached and informed Henry that he had to pop out for a while. Henry reminded him that he had a job to do later. The choir was coming to the end of their song, so Patsy went back upon stage to make ready for the next act. Henry then made his way to stand by Myfannwy, the Bidders and Sofie.

Asgard walked over to join them and when he was next to Sofie she began taking the cabbage bits off his shoulders and out of his pockets.

Sofie then turned to Cynthia. 'Joe is playing well, Cynthia.' She replied that by the look on his face he certainly was. John pointed out that it was not surprising given that he had Claire as company. Myfannwy was the first of the group to compliment Asgard on his juggling but he replied that he had not been at his best.

Cynthia corrected him. 'To me Asgard it was perfection. Four cabbages in the air at the same time. I was impressed and I will be telling the folks back home that's for sure.'

The choir finished singing and Patsy tapped the microphone again.

'Ladies and gentlemen. Could I have your attention please?' The hall fell quite silent. 'Thank you. I am sure you will agree that the children have done us proud tonight.' Another round of applause went round the room. 'And thanks to Joe down there on the piano.' Joe received his applause. 'We are going to take a break now from the singing to allow the children to enjoy our next special visitors.'

Patsy asked the children to leave the stage and group together at the front of the hall. When the children had assembled in the designated area Patsy spoke again.

'Ladies and gentlemen. Our special guest tonight is Walton.' Dalton and Terrence were off stage and hidden behind a curtain. Dalton shouted out that his name was Dalton and not Walton. Patsy duly apologised.

'That's okay Pastie.' This brought about the biggest laugh of the evening so far, and Kingsley shouted hoorah. Gwendoline did not clip him around the ear. It was after all Christmas Eve.

'Touché, Dalton. Dalton, if you would like to come out and join the children in the hall.' There was no response. 'Dalton?' Still no response was forthcoming. 'Perhaps children Dalton needs a round of applause. The children clapped. When the clapping had subsided, it was Terrence that put his head around the curtain. There was no sign of Dalton.

'Sorry about this. Dalton is just putting his elf outfit on.' Terry disappeared back behind the curtain. It was Dalton that spoke next.

'I told you that I am not wearing that elf costume. It itches. You have starched it too much.'

'You are wearing it!' Terry insisted.

'On one condition!' Dalton stated.

'What is the condition, Dalton?'

Dalton in a shy voice replied. 'I'll do it if Pastie gives me a kiss.'

'She won't if you keep calling her that. Her name is Patsy.'

'Sorry Patsy. I forgot. Can I have a kiss?'

Patsy turned to the children. 'What do you think children? Shall I give Dalton a kiss?' The children as one shouted out that she should, and Patsy agreed. She asked him to come out from behind the curtain. Dalton and Terrence came out of the wings and stood by Patsy, whereupon Patsy gave Dalton a peck on the cheek. The children giggled and clapped.

They giggled even more when Dalton declared that it had been nice. Dalton turned his head toward Terry. 'I bet you're jealous now, aren't you?' This was the prompt for Patsy to give Terry a peck on the cheek. Patsy stepped back, watched closely by Dalton. Dalton then turned his head back to look at Terry.

'You've just got to be in on the act, haven't you, Terrence?'

Patsy intervened. 'Ladies, gentlemen and children, put your hands together for Terry and Dalton'. Before the applause was forthcoming however Dalton coughed.

'It's Dalton and Terrence.' he pointed out.

Patsy corrected her introduction. 'Ladies and gentlemen. Dalton and Terrence!' The round of applause that followed accompanied Dalton and Terrence as they left the stage to take up their position in front of the children. Within moments they were enthralling the children and many of the adults with their routine. Patsy took a welcome break.

As Henry was talking to John and Cynthia the three entrepreneurs from the village passed them. Henry stopped them to introduce them to his guests. 'I would like to introduce you three to our American guests. John, Cynthia I would like to introduce Bill the butcher, Bryn the baker and.' He was interrupted by John.

'Don't tell me, Henry. Let me guess. It's Chris the candlestick maker?' The reply was not what John expected. 'No! I am Frank the Post. Chris left the village last year!'

A few yards away Patsy was talking to Joe, Gerald and the twins. 'Have any of you seen Maggie? She is on in a few minutes.' They said that they had not seen her for a while. Claire suggested that she was just off somewhere practicing.

'That was a nice routine with the ventriloquist, reverend.'

Gerald complimented. How long did it take you to rehearse that?'

'About two hours. Dalton kept telling me elf jokes.'

Elizabeth asked her how she managed to get through it. Patsy replied. 'Terry put a sock in his mouth. Didn't stop him!' Patsy smiled and walked away to find Maggie.

Maggie was in fact in the office at the back of hall practicing with, of all people, Bob.

Both he and Maggie had disappeared earlier from the hall to change into their best attire. Maggie was almost unrecognisable in her silk dress and makeup. She was almost on a par with Elizabeth when she was in the guise of Lady Mirley, almost but not quite! Bob had removed his elf outfit and was now in his best tuxedo. The transformation of both was remarkable.

Maggie looked at Bob. 'Well Bob. They cannot say we don't look the part, isn't it?'

'That's true enough, Maggie.' Bob paused for a moment. 'Maggie?' He paused again. 'You know we have known each other a long time.' Before he could finish his sentence, Maggie interrupted.

'You're not proposing to me Bob. I can't be having that!'

'No. It's not that. There is something I have not told you. To be honest I've been too scared to tell you.'

'Scared? You are not a serial killer, are you? I know! You watch those t.v. soaps, don't you?'

'Don't be daft!' He paused again.

'Spit it out boyo. It is not me that you should fear. My mother! That is the one you should fear. Her face is still scaring cats even today.'

Bob summoned up his courage and said quickly. 'I was born and brought up in Llanelli and so were both my parents. There! I've got it off my chest!'

'My goodness!' replied Maggie, shocked. 'That's taken me back somewhat Bob.' It was her turn to pause. 'On reflection however, I guess you are a decent lad, so I'm thinking that not everyone from Llanelli can be that bad. I forgive you Bob.'

'Thank you. Maggie.'

Bob had just finished thanking Maggie when Frank the Post, carrying his Father Christmas outfit in a case, entered the office. 'My apologies. I did not know anyone was in here.' On seeing it was Bob and Maggie, but not as he had seen them before, his jaw dropped. 'Is that really you Maggie?'

'Of course, it's me Frank! I couldn't be someone else, could I?' She turned to Bob. 'Come on Bob. Let us go and knock them sideways.' Bob and Maggie left the room leaving Frank the Post flabbergasted at what he had just witnessed.

Back in the hall Joe and Henry were deep in conversation. 'Do you think he will come Henry?' Joe emphasised the word he.

'Father Christmas? Yes, I am sure of it. You know what Joe. You sounded just like that voice in that Kevin Costner 'Field of Dreams' when that voice said' build it and they will come' although we are, on this occasion only expecting the one. In any case we have Frank the Post waiting in the back office just in case. He's champing at the bit and just waiting to be called upon if needed.'

What Henry did not realise at that time was that, though now fully regaled in his Father Xmas outfit and beard, Frank had fallen asleep in a chair and was snoring his head off with a regular Ho! Ho! Ho! in between his snores.

Patsy, with microphone in hand, was about to announce that the next act must have had stage nerves and would not be appearing when Maggie shouted out from behind the curtains. 'We are here vicar'. Patsy looked towards the wings where Maggie was giving her the thumbs up. Patsy could not however see Bob.

Patsy tapped the microphone and the room fell silent. 'I am delighted to say that we do have our singing duo here to entertain you. The next act is Maggie and well, her singing partner.' At this point Bob shouted out from the wings that it would be him accompanying Maggie. To say a gasp went around the hall would be an understatement. Maggie and Bob singing together?

Patsy had regained her composure. 'Ladies and gentlemen, here, singing Silent Night in the A Capella style, are our very own Maggie and Bob.'

As Maggie and Bob, microphones in hand, appeared from behind the curtains to take their positions center stage, several small events took place in the hall. Patsy nearly dropped the microphone when she saw how they dressed, Kingsley shouted 'hoorah' for no other reason than he wanted to, people were re-assuring each other that it was really Maggie and Bob, Dalton's jaw dropped with surprise, Myfannwy turned to Henry and commented that it would be incredible if Maggie could sing Silent Night silently, and Ingrid clapped and said, 'Stille Natt is my favourite of all the carols.'

Henry, on hearing this, turned to Myfannwy. 'I hope it still is after this.'

The hall fell silent. Bob looked at Maggie, cleared his throat, and asked Maggie if she was ready. She nodded that she was. They turned to face their audience, all one hundred and thirty-seven of them. Bob began the first verse, with the next lines being sung either alternatively or in chorus.

Not a pin could be heard falling throughout their performance. They sang it beautifully. It was in tune, sung at the right tempo and with feeling. The harmony when they sang the lines together was, as Henry described it later, magical.

Their last line together of 'Christ the Saviour is born' when delivered, brought huge applause and a standing ovation. Gwendoline, on noticing her husband silent and in tears, clipped him around the ear, but this time it was to get him to shout 'hoorah.' This he did as he wiped the tears from his face.

Such was the vibration in the hall's wooden floor when people stamped the floor that the tree even shook. It was Maggie's eagle eyes that noticed this, so she moved to the other side of Bob, further away from the tree.

Maggie and Bob bowed and took two curtain calls. Once completed, Maggie came down to see Aggie and Bob went off to change back into his elf's costume. Patsy had by this time looked upwards. 'Blinking heck, Lord. You hid that well!' Just as she had finished, Dalton and Terrence walked up to her.

Dalton addressed her properly 'Hello Patsy.'

'Hello Dalton. I thought our little routine went down well.'

'I agree. My performance was flawless, and I did not break sweat once.'

'I thought it was a bit wooden, personally.' commented Terry.

Patsy turned to talk to Terrence. 'Thank you, Terry for helping us tonight. The children really took to Dalton.'

Before Terry could reply however, Dalton spoke. 'Well! They would not have come to see Terrence if he had been on his own. Without me he has not got an act.'

'I could have given them a song.' suggested Terry.

'Don't make me laugh. I'll crack my varnish.'

Patsy stepped in as peacemaker. 'Now don't fall out boys. You work well together, and we are grateful this evening for that.' Patsy felt a tap on her shoulder. It was the major. Dalton immediately sat more upright in Terry's arms.

'Attention! Officer on parade.' He commanded, as his hand was raised in salute. The major returned with a salute of his own.

'I'm not interrupting am I Patsy?' the major asked.

'Not at all, Timothy. I didn't think you were going to make it tonight.'

'Change of plan. Thought I would pop in and give you some moral support. I hope you do not mind me asking, but how do your finances allow you to book such a professional singing act. I was at the back of the hall and well, to be honest I got quite emotional.'

Patsy responded by simply saying. 'They were heaven sent!'

Time had flown by and it was now just twenty minutes before Father Christmas was due to arrive. Henry checked with Bob and Gregor that they were ready, and the elves took up their positions on stage. Ingrid was snapping away taking photos of the elves when Myfannwy turned to Sofie.

'Just look at Ingrid. She has been taking photographs all evening. She has a lot of energy.' Then a thought struck her. 'Oh my! Did anyone think to get Ingrid a present from Father Christmas?'

Patsy, who was now standing next to her with the major replied. 'I am sorry to say it never crossed my mind, Myfannwy. Oh dear!' Cynthia asked if there were any surplus presents available, but Patsy confirmed that they had received just enough to cover the other children. She went off to check in the office just in case. Sofie said that Ingrid would understand that she was not from the village and therefore could not expect one. A little while later Patsy returned to confirm that she had not been able to find a present for Ingrid.

CHAPTER FORTY-ONE
FATHER CHRISTMAS

With ten minutes to go Patsy positioned herself in the middle of the stage. 'Ladies and Gentlemen, and in particular children, we have been informed that Father Christmas is close by. Would you children from a line at the bottom of the steps and when we call you, please come up to receive your present off Father Christmas.' The children eagerly lined up.

Ingrid by this time had joined her parents and they explained that she was not eligible to have a present off Father Christmas that evening. Ingrid replied that she never thought she would be having one.

Henry was having a final check with Bob and Gregor when there was a loud thud on the village hall roof. The room once again fell silent amidst an atmosphere of excitement and anticipation.

Henry instructed Gregor to get ready with his switches, Maggie commented that she hoped it was not her mother, and in the back-office Frank the Post woke up with a start and fell off his chair.

Within an instant Father Christmas appeared from behind the curtains, laughing and waving, and with his customary Ho! Ho! Ho! The elves stepped forward to greet him and escort him to the sleigh. Father Christmas sat down in the sleigh and burst into another round of Ho! Ho! Ho! Gregor pushed his first button and the sleigh at once lit up, to the delight of all in the hall. Henry exclaimed, 'Thank goodness!'

Gregor announced to Henry that he was activating the second switch. Rudolph's nose, however, did not light up. Henry expressed his disappointment at Gregor and suggested that he had not screwed the bulb in properly. Henry was in the process of admonishing both Gregor and Bob when Myfannwy tugged on his sleeve and told him to look up at the stage.

Father Christmas had climbed out of the sleigh and was standing looking at Rudolph's not so red nose. He looked over in the direction of Bob and Gregor, tweaked his nose, and the bulb lit up bright red. Cynthia declared, 'And the magic goes on!'

Father Christmas took up his position back in the sleigh. Bob turned to Henry and suggested that Gregor should have tweaked his nose and not used the switch. Henry just looked at him in disbelief, but least he was now happy that all the lights were now working.

Up on the stage the elves which included Eddie, Gillian and Bob were now in the process of calling the children up onto the stage to receive their presents. The children included Jeremy Thorncroft and his new-found friend Jason Cartwright. They went up on stage together. The process of giving out the presents proceeded until the last child had received a present.

Bob had come down from the stage and confirmed to Patsy that every child had received a present and there were no more presents left in the sleigh. Myfannwy, on hearing this, looked over to Ingrid to check she was okay, but she was fine. She was standing with Terry and Dalton, laughing at his antics.

It was now Henry that tugged his wife's sleeve. 'Look up at the stage, Myfannwy.' He instructed. Up on the stage Father Christmas was beckoning to Ingrid to come up to see him. She was unsure at first whether it was her that he meant, but Terry confirmed that it was. Ingrid climbed the steps and walked over to the sleigh.

Father Christmas reached down into the sleigh and withdrew a Christmas present with her name on it. Myfannwy turned to Patsy and thanked her for finding one but Patsy re-iterated that she had not been able to find one. This was as big a mystery to her as anyone. Cynthia turned to husband and said, 'John, we are definitely coming back here next year!'

Ingrid and Father Christmas chatted to each other for a couple of minutes and when they had finished Ingrid rejoined her parents. Father Christmas, with a big wave and a huge laugh, hopped off stage and disappeared behind the curtains. One or two of the more adventurous children went up on stage to try and find him, but he was nowhere to be found.

Maggie who had been watching everything that had been going on approached Patsy. 'That Father Christmas is like a Welsh Lone Ranger. Nobody knows his real identity and he disappears before you know it. I bet you Tonto is on the roof looking after the reindeer.'

Patsy chuckled as she replied. 'And I suppose Silver and Scout are two of his reindeer, eh? I think we do know his real identity, Maggie.'

'Who, the lone ranger? Maggie asked.

'No, our real visitor. You know. Him. Father Christmas.'

'I knew that, isn't it?' With that Maggie went off to find Aggie and to check on Mr. Cole.

Henry and Myfannwy had by now joined their daughters and Gerald at the piano. Asgard and Sofie, with Ingrid holding on to both her camera and her present joined them. John and Cynthia were across the hall talking to Terry and Dalton and Joe made sure that he took the opportunity of having a chat with Jeremy and his parents. He then went over to talk to his parents.

Much was being discussed by the group at the piano when Myfannwy commented that this, she felt, had been the best Christmas ever. Her two daughters were home for Christmas and the Larsens and the Bidders had been wonderful guests. Maggie and Aggie were passing at the time Myfannwy was saying this.

'Bidder? Did you say Bidder, Myfannwy?' Maggie asked, inquisitively. 'You know that is my maiden name. isn't it?'

'I never knew, Maggie. What a co-incidence!' replied Myfannwy.

Henry joined the conversation. 'I might regret asking this but where did they hail from Maggie?'

'Tongwynlais. They were very well known there.' Came back the reply.

Henry was intrigued. 'Did any of your ancestors fight in the boxing booths by any chance, Maggie?'

'Absolutely they did. It was a way to make some extra money, wasn't it? One of my ancestors was particularly handy with his fists. He was known as Billy the....'

Henry stopped her before she could finish. 'Billy the Bash?'

Maggie looked at him in amazement at Henry knowing the name. 'You've heard of him then?'

'I have indeed, Maggie!' With that Maggie and Aggie went off to find Aggie's husband.

Myfannwy turned to face her husband. 'You know what that means Henry, don't you?'

Henry spoke slowly back to her 'That John and Maggie are cousins, albeit second or third cousins but they are indeed related! Well, jigger me!'

'Are you going to tell John?' Myfannwy enquired.

'You bet I am. Come on.'

Claire and Patsy, who had been listening with great interest, expressed their wish to accompany him when he told the Bidders. They were not going to miss out on that revelation.

Later that evening only Bob and Patsy remained in the hall to lock up. The lights on the sleigh and the main lights in the hall were turned off leaving just the moonlight through the windows to cast light into the hall. Patsy and Bob exited the hall, Patsy locked the door, and they went their separate ways.

All was not over inside the hall, however. Ten minutes after Bob and Patsy had left, and all was calm and peaceful, Rudolph's nose lit up. Five minutes later the Christmas tree fell over. Christmas Eve had come to its conclusion.

CHAPTER FORTY-TWO
THREE ELVES A-CHATTING

Christmas Day had arrived and everyone in the lodge had risen early to enjoy the full day of festivities. Maggie and Bob joined them in the morning for an extremely enjoyable breakfast. Christmas presents were exchanged, games were played, and Joe entertained on the piano.

Bob and Maggie were persuaded to repeat their performance of Silent Night, Ingrid captured the moments on camera, and a few drinks were consumed.

Later that afternoon they were enjoying a magnificent Christmas dinner that had been prepared by Claire, Myfannwy and Joe. Unbeknown to them however, they were being spied upon through the windows of the dining room. Outside, sitting on a bench, were Eddie, Gillian and Terry. Terry was cradling Dalton. Each one had the words 'REAL ELVES DO NOT FEEL THE COLD' printed on their jackets.

Gillian was the first to speak. 'Do you think they knew who we really were, Eddie?'

He replied, 'Perhaps one did but the others, no.'

'Well, I for one, am glad to be back in my normal clothes. Those elf clothes don't half itch the wood grain.' Dalton declared.

Terry was looking at the turkey that was positioned proudly at the one end of the table, and which was now being carved by

Asgard. Next to the turkey there were three large dishes of cabbage. 'Just have a look at the size of that turkey!'

Dalton responded. 'That's big enough to be an ostrich!'

'I think the big man will be pleased with our efforts.' Gillian remarked.

'Talking of the boss, we'd better make tracks.' Eddie pointed to inside the Cwtch. 'We'd best leave those guys to the rest of their day and we've got to be somewhere else anyway.' He looked up at the sky. 'Hey boss! How about some white stuff?' Snowflakes began to fall. The Cwtch Inn Christmas was not yet over but their assignment was.

They disappeared in a sparkle.

In the months that followed:

The Cwtch Inn re-opened in the Spring with all its chalets fully functional and Henry and Myfannwy still at the helm.

Joe and Claire were married in Pontynant with Maggie as matron of honour.

Elizabeth was a great success in her role as Lady Mirley. The play toured the U.K.

Claire remained at the Cwtch as joint head chef alongside Joe.

John and Cynthia pledged to visit the Cwtch every year at Christmas.

The police did eventually catch up with Asgard before he went back to Norway over the cabbage incident, but it came to nothing. P.C. Green was more interested in how Asgard could grow such big cabbages. The Larsens were visitors to the lodge in the summer.

Maggie formed a partnership with Bob to raise ostriches. A frequent visitor to their paddocks was Jeremy who jokingly always called the ostriches turkeys.

Maggie's mother came to visit regularly but never on her broomstick. Bob arranged with Henry that he could borrow the minibus to taxi her back and for.

Eddie, Gillian, Terry and Dalton never returned to the Cwtch as far as anyone was aware, but at the next elf competition there was a suspicion by Henry that there were real elves in amongst the list of hopefuls.

Patsy remained at the church and married the major.

Father Christmas continues to be a regular visit to the hall and Frank the Post hung up his Father Christmas costume for good. He did however become an elf.

THE END (ISN'T IT?)

Printed in Great Britain
by Amazon

59041453R00108